D0362852

SNOWBOUND

Private enquiry agent Carson Banner
has been hired to track down Julian
Prince's missing daughters — Candice,
who has eloped with the no-good
swindler Bill Saxon; and Ruth, who
refused to let her younger sister go
off alone with strangers. As a snow-
storm out of Canada blows its way
south across Dakota land, Banner
must find the party before harm comes
to the girls — or the blizzards kill
them all . . .

LOGAN WINTERS

SNOWBOUND

Complete and Unabridged

LINFORD
Leicester

First published in Great Britain in 2014 by
Robert Hale Limited
London

First Linford Edition
published 2017
by arrangement with
Robert Hale
an imprint of
The Crowood Press
Wiltshire

A catalogue record for this book is available
from the British Library.

ISBN 978–1–4448–3417–8

Published by
F. A. Thorpe (Publishing)
Anstey, Leicestershire

Set by Words & Graphics Ltd.
Anstey, Leicestershire
Printed and bound in Great Britain by
T. J. International Ltd., Padstow, Cornwall

This book is printed on acid-free paper

1

It was not an easy time for traveling. The snow had been blowing hard for days as a storm out of Canada made its way south across the Dakota land. The old pine trees which had seen hundreds of such storms huddled together shivering in their white blankets. Carson found the wagon on the slope leading up to the crest of Tomahawk Ridge. Why anyone heading out for Oregon would have chosen the high pass at this time of the year was beyond Carson. But then, it was foolish to try taking any route toward the Oregon country once the first snows had settled in. These people had been determined to make fools of themselves.

The covered wagon was slumped to the ground, settled on a broken rear wheel like a beast that had died in its tracks. The wind whipping through the pine forest flapped the canvas top of the wagon.

The northern sky was colored that strange blue-black that presages an approaching storm. Carson glanced that way unhappily. It would snow again, and this one, at this time of year, could be much worse. A smothering blizzard that would bury the land, break forests, allow movement for no living thing.

Matters were bad enough as they stood. The runaways had gotten themselves into a bad position, and Carson Banner was being sucked into it after them. Where could they have gone now? They had the horse team, of course, but if they had a bit of sense, they would know they needed to find shelter. The only town that Carson had heard of within a hundred miles was Tumble Oaks, if that small collection of huts clinging to the side of a mountain like a dying insect could be called a town.

Carson sighed, gave up trying to outthink the travelers, and got back to work. He first looked in the back of the crippled wagon, noticing the load of household furniture and an iron stove which had shifted to one side of the bed. There were no blankets, no personal items that he could see . . . and no food. There was a flour barrel. They couldn't have carried it, nor could he.

Turning next to the snow-covered earth around the broken wagon, he searched for prints — of horses or of man. There were neither. A later dusting of snow had covered any sign of passage. Remounting, Carson continued on his way, surveying the long land. To the north were the high blue mountains. To the south were the lowland valleys where Carson himself would have gone if he had sensed a blizzard. But these travelers were not that sort — they had started west, and west they would continue. Perhaps they felt they would be gaining time that way; instead they would probably be losing their lives.

Greed had warped their thinking utterly.

There was no discernible trail westward, only places where the gaps between the big pines allowed passage. Passable for a lone man on a horse — what would they have done if they had managed to get this far with a wagon and team? The going would have been insufferably slow.

Now and then Carson passed one of the few dormant oak trees that stood on the high slopes. These raised supplicating black limbs to the turbulent sky, casting wrought-iron silhouettes. In one of these a lone crow perched, seeming perfectly at home, yet baffled by the weather. The bird turned its head, but did not make a sound or take to the frigid sky as Carson rode slowly past, his gray horse making almost no sound against the earth, which was of compacted pine needles beneath the blanket of new snow.

There was no smell but the almost overpowering scent of the pines, no sound but the wind in the treetops, no sight but the long forest. Carson reined in abruptly, a little sharply so that the gray tossed its head in annoyance.

Carson swung down and went to the lone bright spot the bleak day held. Squatting down next to the ridge of snow, he examined it more closely. It was the crimson of blood, or something very like blood. Out here, blood seemed the only possibility for the stain. It was fresh to have remained bright and not absorbed by the snow.

Carson rose, dusted his gloved hands together and again studied the ground around him. There were no boot prints, no signs of horses having passed this way. Of course the blood could have belonged to a wild thing. Carson had no evidence to support his feeling that it was human.

He returned to his uniquely colored horse. It was a gray, but its entire right rear leg was white. Nature had been enjoying itself on that day. The horse was unique, and probably too recognizable. That thought had occurred to Carson Banner before; yet he was fond of the beast, too fond of it to trade mounts so that some sharp-eyed lookout couldn't call out: 'Here comes Carson Banner!'

Well, a man gets used to things even if they are not the wisest choices.

Half a mile on, Carson's path was crossed by a timber wolf which glared at him with hungry yellow eyes. It slunk past him, looking up now and then. The old animal had a scruffy coat which should have been filled out by now for the coming winter. It was a hungry, prowling wretch. A lone wolf without a den to return to. Probably it had briefly considering trying to take the horse down, but by itself, with a human on its back it had decided against it.

'Good luck to you, old-timer,' Carson said with a slight smile. Game was getting hard to come by with the settling of winter, but he knew the wolf could probably survive on squirrels, birds' eggs, snakes and weasels with any luck.

Which turned Carson's thoughts to his own survival. He had a minimum of supplies in a burlap sack behind his saddle, but the gray horse needed to be fed if he were to survive. And both of them needed shelter from the storm if it turned out to be as heavy as he suspected it would be. Men he could fight, wolves he could fight, but there was no fighting back against a full-blown blizzard in the north country.

The squat, shadowed shape suddenly revealed itself through a gap in the trees. Carson squinted that way.

A lonely, broken-down cabin stood among the trees high in this isolated land. Carson hesitated momentarily and then started his horse that way. He rode toward the little shanty, the cold wind now full in his face. A single chattering gray squirrel bounded along a pine limb briefly following Carson.

There were no horses near the cabin, which sat in a small clearing surrounded by looming pines and cedar trees. No smoke rose from the iron stovepipe in the center of its roof. It must have been a prospector's cabin, Carson thought, or a fur trapper's. Someone who long ago had cut himself off from civilization and its wicked, venial ways. A man — for what woman would choose to live alone in an isolated place like this? — who had learned to support himself with only his two hands and asked for nothing else but survival and peace of mind from the world.

Ordinarily Carson would have hallooed the house, but the shack seemed to have been long vacant, and the people he was following might take it as invitation to start shooting if they happened to be holed up inside.

Approaching, Carson rode with one hand on his holstered Colt revolver. He still could not be sure that someone wasn't waiting, watching. The shack had been constructed without windows out of necessity, and so Carson felt fairly safe in swinging down at the rear of the shack where he dropped the reins to his gray horse and slipped his rifle from its scabbard. He started warily toward the front of the little place and then halted as he heard a small, muffled sound from within. A few stray snowflakes had drifted against his face and Carson brushed them away as he paused, listening intently.

The sound came again: small, plaintive, miserable.

It couldn't be faked; someone inside was distressed and hurt. With determination overcoming caution, Carson rounded the corner of the cabin and strode to the door of the low building, his rifle at the ready.

The plank door, hanging unevenly on leather hinges, stood partially open. Carson toed it farther with the toe of his boot and entered with his rifle leveled.

The shack's interior was dark, gloomy, rank and disordered. It smelled of a hundred dead fires, burnt tobacco, old hides and singed fur. There was a heavy odor of unwashed man, guttered candles and grease. His first impression was that the place needed to stand open, airing out for a few days and then be burned to the ground.

'You'll have to kill me,' a low,

whimpering voice said from the darkness.

'Relax,' Carson Banner replied to the unseen man. 'I'm not here to kill anybody or to cause you any trouble.'

Gradually, as his eyes adjusted to the gloom, Carson was able to make out the huddled figure of the man who had spoken to him. He was old, narrow, sitting on a ragged mattress on a corner bed. His knees were drawn up, his arms looped around them. His face was turned toward Carson, and it showed only desperation.

'What's happened here?' Carson asked, retreating toward the door and swinging it open wider to let in more light and to let out a little of the accumulated stink. He seated himself on a roughly made puncheon chair which had been upended on the floor and sat facing the narrow-faced, whiskered man. There was an unhealthiness in the stranger's eyes and in the way he moved.

'You don't know?' the man challenged before breaking into a coughing fit which seemed to hurt him because he folded his arm across his lower ribs.

'If I did I wouldn't have asked you. How am I supposed to know? I just this minute arrived.'

'You're not one of them, then,' the old man said, seeming to relax just a little. There was still a look of fear in his dark eyes, which were arched over with heavy brows.

'I'm not one of anybody,' Carson said, 'and I don't know who you mean,' although he suspected that he did.

'They beat me up pretty bad,' the old man said in a weak voice. He was trying very hard to swing his legs to the side of the bed so that he could sit upright. Carson could see the wince of pain on the whiskered face.

'Why?' Carson wanted to know.

'Why?' the old man echoed. He had gotten his booted feet to the floor. Now he sat with his hands on his knees, looking up at Carson with miserable eyes. There was enough cold light spraying around the room now through

11

the door that Carson could see that the place had been ravaged.

'They said I wasn't co-operating with them,' the old man said, 'although I think it was done mostly for fun, or maybe to prove something to themselves.'

'Two men?' Carson asked. 'One very big and tall, the other much smaller?'

The old man's face tightened. 'I thought you said you weren't with them,' he said.

'I'm not and I wasn't. I'm on their trail, though. I mean to find them.'

'You do know who they are,' the old man said.

'I do know that, yes.'

The injured man nodded toward the rifle which lay across Carson Banner's lap. 'Are you meaning to kill them when you find them?'

'If it has to come to that, and knowing them I figure it might.'

The old man nodded. He began looking across the cabin at the ransacked interior. 'They took all of my food — coffee, salt, corn meal, bacon . . . ' he continued as he looked around the room, taking a mental inventory. 'You know what it means to lose all that to a man who's getting ready to winter down?'

'I think I do,' Carson replied. Once the snows set in there was no way to replace any commodities.

'It's the next thing to murder,' his host answered in a strangled voice. 'And I ain't even got a mule now.'

'They took your animal too?'

'You bet they did! Old Sally was a good old mule.' He was briefly reflective. 'It's the same as murdering a man!' he repeated in case Carson had not grasped the full import of his words.

'I suppose they didn't want you following them.'

'And you can bet I would have — even though they took my rifle as well. I would have found some way to settle with them.'

Carson rose. He had pity for the old

man but did not care to run through his sorrows one by one. 'I can fix you something to eat out of my grub,' Carson offered.

'Would you do that for me, stranger? It would be a blessing. More of one would be when you do find those men, to kill them where they stand.'

2

Over a poor meal which was only beans with shaved jerky added — all Carson could easily prepare and all he was willing to share with his own needs being long — they talked between mouthfuls.

The old man's name was Elijah Tuttle. He had been alone in these mountains for four years. He did occasional gold panning and fur trapping to support himself, and rode his mule into Tumble Oaks — a two-day trip over rough country — to sell his furs to traders and use what little gold dust he had collected to pay for the necessities to survive a winter up in the tall timber.

It wasn't much of a life, Elijah ('Call me Lige') admitted, and not many men could have stomached it for long, but it suited him and his solitary ways.

'I have a guest come by maybe twice, three times a year. Mostly they just tell me new stories about how bad things have gotten out in what they call civilization. I welcome them all in and usually break out my single bottle of whiskey that I keep for those occasions.

'So, I was kind of glad to see these people arriving — especially since they had the two women with them. I don't like women, can't live with them, but I do appreciate the sight of someone in skirts.'

Carson nodded.

'There were three men, weren't there?' he asked Lige.

'Must have been, though I never saw another one. There had to be someone holding that team of four horses they came with. Yes, I suspect there had to be another one, but I only saw the two. And the two women.'

'One of them very young, the other a little older, but both pretty, dark-haired?' Carson inquired.

'That's them,' Lige replied. Then his

eyes narrowed shrewdly. 'You seem to know a lot about this party for someone who isn't one of them. Do you mind telling me how?' he asked, pushing his empty plate away.

'No,' Carson said. 'They're thieves, all of them.'

'Aren't they? Those two drank my whiskey with me and then took what was left of the bottle away with them. After they had raided my provisions and beaten me up.'

'They're not worth much,' Carson admitted. 'Their thieving is why I'm looking for them.'

'Then you're some sort of lawman?' Lige suggested.

'No.' Carson pushed his own plate away and leaned back in his chair. 'I work for a man called John Dancer — does the name mean anything to you?'

'Not a thing.' Lige shrugged apologetically.

'How could it?' Carson said, realizing the circumstances of Elijah Tuttle's present life. 'John Dancer runs a small agency which specializes in tracking those the law can't find or whose victims don't want them prosecuted. A father whose wayward son has been embezzling family funds, for example. A banker whose short-changing teller is his wife's brother. When no complaint has been made, the law can't do a thing.'

'So — you're like detectives?' Lige suggested.

'Not that either. Aren't detectives the ones who are supposed to solve crimes? No, we usually know who the guilty ones are. The injured parties contact us and tell us all they weren't willing to tell the local sheriff. Of course, not wishing to send your son to prison for taking your purse doesn't mean that you don't want your coin back, and the kid to learn a lesson from it,' Carson said.

'So, that's what we have been formed to do. People bring their complaints to us in confidence and we try to handle them privately.'

'You ask me, those two men could stand a prison term. What else have they done, and what do the women have to do with it?'

What they had done was easily told, but not easily understood as Carson had gotten it from Julian Prince. The two women were his daughters. The younger, Candice, had fallen for a no-good swindler, William Saxon, who had come to the Nine-Slash-Seven ranch apparently for the specific purpose of tricking her into marrying him and convincing her that they would need some of her father's money for the trip to Oregon where he said he had a small ranch.

The old man, Julian Prince, was having no talk of marriage for his daughter, who was only sixteen. Besides, he was convinced that Bill Saxon was just no good. Of course the girl didn't believe that, as no young girl in love would. She cried and argued until Prince gave in just a little. He said he would talk to them when he got back from the cattle-buying trip he had planned just to satisfy the girl.

Saxon gave Prince two days before he

cracked the old man's office safe. There was no way of knowing if Candice knew about that part of the plan or not. That evening a man named Lou Weathers — the big man Elijah Tuttle had seen — arrived on the Nine-Slash-Seven (or 9/7 as the brand read) with a covered wagon. Bill Saxon and Candice loaded it hastily. They were going to Oregon to be married. With the old man's money in Saxon's purse.

'There were two women,' Lige interrupted at this point.

'Yes, the other was Candice's older sister, Ruth. Ruth said she would not let her sister go off into the wilds with a couple of men who were virtual strangers.'

Bill Saxon refused to take Ruth with them, but Candice pleaded with him until he relented. Lou Weathers had no objection. His wink at Saxon indicated that he might just get 'married' himself along the way.

'The old man couldn't have known all this to tell you,' Lige commented.

'There was a maid at the house, and a yardman. They told Julian Prince everything they had seen and heard.'

'You said there was also a third man,' Lige persisted. Carson nodded.

'I don't know if there was for sure or what he was doing here; them two sure hadn't invited him along.'

He was a kid named Wesley Short. He'd hired on as a cowhand not six months before, but had his eyes on Candice before he had swung down from his pony. He was near Candice's age and there weren't many other youngsters around. He must have figured that they'd eventually get together. The arrival of William Saxon changed that, crushing the kid's dream.

'I think he just decided to follow along,' Carson said.

Lige nodded his head. The movement seemed to hurt him. 'The romantic type.'

'So it seems.'

'Then, this Julian Prince, he contacted you folks to bring back his money, the girls.'

'That's it. The old man had broken his leg while on his trip, and anyway he didn't think it was fair to ask his men to ride out in this weather. That's not what they were hired on to do, and no one could know how long the hunt would take.'

'But time don't matter that much to you boys, I take it.'

'The only thing that matters is getting the job done,' Carson told him. 'People would quit hiring us if we didn't get results.'

'But your boss — this John Dancer — didn't see fit to come himself.'

'Mr Dancer has a couple of other important jobs going on right now,' Carson said, 'and as I explained to Julian Prince, just because you hire the Pinkerton Detectives for a job, that doesn't mean you'll find Allan Pinkerton himself on your doorstep.'

'No, I guess not,' Lige said, rubbing his long, whiskered chin.

'The only issue I have with time

meaning much right now is the weather. If those fools are out in it when a real blizzard hits, they'll all die in these mountains: the money they've taken can't purchase their lives.'

There was a long silence between the men. Outside the sky was darkening; it was growing late and Carson suspected that a fresh storm was contributing to the darkness.

Lige muttered something, shook his head as if reconsidering it and then looked up with watery eyes at Carson Banner. He cleared his throat and said:

'I know where they're headed.'

'What do you mean?' Carson asked.

'I know where they're headed to wait out the winter storms. I told them that I knew a place and they left off beating me when I told them. Of course they said they'd kill me if I told anyone else, but then I kinda figure you've already saved my life and I owe you for that.'

'You told them someplace they could hole up?' Carson asked with surprise.

The old man slowly nodded his head.

'A man gets tired of being beat up,' Elijah said. He fingered his split, swollen lips.

'All right,' Carson sighed. 'Now suppose you tell me about it?'

Lige did, but unwillingly, perhaps fearing his attackers would find out and come back to extract vengeance.

'You know Sterling March?' Elijah asked.

'No. I'm not from around here, remember?'

'I thought you might have heard about him anyway. You see his name everywhere you go.' Carson nodded and waited. Outside the day was already growing late. He had closed a lot of ground following these people as they guided their slow-moving wagon westward, but now that he was nearly on their heels, he wanted to finish the job as quickly as possible. Before the storms came, if possible. Lige continued.

'Old March, he came out early into these mountains and struck it rich. His mines were turning out high-grade gold ore by the hundreds of tons, and not so

24

very long ago.' Carson knew this was all leading somewhere, and waited impatiently.

'About five years ago March gave it up and sold out to one of those mining combines. Well, he knew, and the mining company should have known, that the gold seam was about played out. The combine worked on the mine for a couple of more years and then gave it up — it was costing them too much to haul the ore out for what they were making off it.

'Sterling March, he was one smart man. He was brawny, but he worked as much with his brain as he did with shoulders and arms. What March did was find himself another business to go into with the profit he'd made mining. He started manufacturing beer on a large scale. That probably made him more money than the gold mine ever did.'

Carson Banner, who had not asked to hear the man's life story, shifted his feet impatiently and frowned. Lige

25

caught the hint and held up a hand.

'I know. I just thought it might help you to understand matters. Sterling March built himself a house up here, not far from the old gold strike. It's got fifty rooms in it, if you can credit that.'

'Fifty . . . '

'Old March had just a wheelbarrow full of money to spend, and it pleased his old woman after living for years in a prospector's cabin or a camp tent. The house is not far from here. There's a staff to maintain it living in it.'

'And Sterling March is there?' Carson asked.

'The old man!' Lige laughed. 'I told you he was smart, didn't I? Too smart to spend a winter in these mountains when the blizzards started to form. Spring, summer, it's a beautiful countryside but it produces some miserable winters. No, he's got him another house down to the south somewhere — Denver, I think, near his brewery. Every year him and his wife pack up and head down that way.'

Carson tried to cut Lige's rambling tale short. 'You sent those people over there, to the March house?'

'Yes, sir,' Lige answered. He paused, coughed long and hard, and continued. 'Sterling March was never one to turn a man in need of shelter away when the storms hit. With those two — Saxon and Weathers — having two women with them, the folks at the house are bound to find them rooms to stay for a while.'

'Sounds like a sort of free hotel,' Carson commented.

'It's nothing like one. One year my shack got near blown away and I stayed there for a while. They've got rules like no hotel ever had, Carson. If you break the rules, why they just throw you out in the storm to repent.'

'Sounds harsh.'

'A man's got to protect his home, and if he invites guests in and they don't know how to behave, why then, you show them the door.'

'You're right,' Carson said, rising. 'I

don't suppose shooting another guest is allowed there.'

'Highly frowned on,' Elijah agreed.

'If that's where the thieves are, that's where I'm going. Do you think I've got time to make it before nightfall?'

'If you don't waste any time about it.'

'Then get to your feet, Lige. We're ready to move.'

'Me!' Elijah Tuttle said with a combination of fear and surprise. 'Why would I want to go tracking down the men who threatened to kill me if they saw me again?' Lige shook his head, holding his eyes closed. 'Not me, Carson, I'm too old and beat up to even try fighting them off again. They got me once; I won't give them a second chance at it.'

'All right,' Carson said, looking around the ravaged hut. 'You make your own decision, Lige. The way I see it though, your only two choices are to come along with me or to sit here waiting for the winter storms to settle in while you slowly starve to death.'

3

It wasn't easy getting himself and Elijah Tuttle mounted on his gray horse, but they managed it and Carson started out in the direction indicated by Lige toward the Sterling March mansion where they assumed Candice and Ruth Prince had been taken by their captors. Or was 'captors' the right word? Candice seemed to have fallen prey to some childish fantasy that her man had come to rescue her from a life of boredom and take her away to her own realm where she would reign as princess. She certainly did not consider herself to be a captive. At least not yet.

Maybe seeing the way Bill Saxon and Lou Weathers had treated Lige had opened her eyes. Who knew? Even though Carson was still a young man, he could barely remember being six-teen. And, he was sure that even then he did not know how sixteen-year-old girls' minds worked.

As he rode on, guiding the stolid, overloaded gray horse, the icy wind was in his face. They passed among the tall pines and an occasional clump of snow was loosened from the high branches by the wind along with dry twigs and pine cones to fall heavily to the ground. The going was miserable, the trail uneven. It must have been worse for Lige, who hung on to Carson almost desperately.

'What are you going to tell them?' Lige had inquired fearfully.

'Who? The people at March's house? No one at all there could possibly know me. I'll just tell them I happened across you hurt and alone, and with the weather settling in, I brought you over here. You told me that you'd stayed here before in an emergency, and I thought it worth a try.'

'I guess that'll work — for you,' Lige said glumly. 'If those boys are up there, they won't be happy to see my face again.'

'You said they had strict house rules at the March house,' Carson replied. 'I don't think they'll put up with any rough action there. Besides, you've got me.'

'Do I?' Lige asked. 'Are you really on my side, Carson?'

'Well, at least I'm not against you,' Carson answered, unsure of what the question really meant.

They rode on for another hour through the gloom of the solemn pines and the settling darkness of the mountain sundown until Carson thought he could see the shoulder of a tall building to the north.

'Is that it?' he asked Lige, pointing that way.

'What else?'

Yes, what else could it be, standing stark and bulky in the northern woods, but the house Sterling March had built to please his wife or as a monument to himself?

'Are you ready to approach it?' Carson asked.

'It's another of those situations where

I've got little choice,' Lige said through chattering teeth. 'We go up there or I slowly freeze to death out here in the open.'

That much was true — for the both of them. The wind was starting to howl dangerously. The pines swayed in agitated unison. Far in the distance Carson saw lightning spark among the dark wool of the storm clouds, illuminating them briefly, and seconds later the low grumbling of thunder reached them.

Oh, yes, it was time to get under shelter or face a very bad night indeed.

Emerging from the forest they came upon a deliberately cleared parcel of land thirty acres in size at a guess. The house itself was a brooding thing, two stories high along its great length. The roof was of slate, presumably to lessen the chance of destruction by fire.

Carson could see an equally imposing barn beyond and behind the house. It must have had stalls equal to the number of guests the house could shelter.

Could Sterling March have ever expected to have fifty guests arrive at this remote location? Maybe it had been one of his wife's dreams to have a grand ball in the house and greet her many guests some summer day. It was not a logical expectation, but then, a woman's dreams seldom are.

''Bout the third window along downstairs, someone is watching us,' Elijah Tuttle said.

'I saw him,' Carson replied, guiding the horse through the gloom and steady wind toward the big house. Someone had drawn back a sheer curtain a little to peer out at them. Well, that was hardly suspicious. Someone wanted to know who was coming; looking out a window beat getting dressed and coming outside into the cold to find out who it was.

Yet they had no friends here — only a group of people they had never met, and a gang of thieving bullies. For now Carson knew he had to get the two of them out of the cold and find a bed for

Lige, who had just about had it.

It had begun to snow again, lightly, like a preamble to the storm by the time they reached the front door — or rather one of the two front doors to the huge house. A scattering of flakes wind-whipped against them, dusted their hats and shoulders. Halting the gray horse at the black iron hitch rail, Carson managed to twist around in the saddle enough so that he could grip Lige's arms and keep him from falling as he slid from the horse's back to the ground.

A small dark figure appeared from nowhere and rushed at them. Carson stiffened, prepared for anything.

'Yes, I get 'im, I get 'im!' the dark apparition said. Scuttling toward Carson he grabbed the reins to the gray horse. 'Yes, I get 'im, boss, I get 'im,' the small creature said again.

The little man was very dark, perhaps an Indian. One eye seemed to look in a different direction from the other. Of course Sterling March would have employed a stable boy, Carson reflected, and of course the man would have been among those who stayed at the house throughout the winter. Where else would someone like the crooked little man go; where else could he possibly wish to be?

Carson had swung down; now he watched the swarthy man lead his gray along the length of the house and then toward the horse barn. He didn't like letting the gray go, but he wasn't really up to taking care of its feeding and grooming on this night.

'What are we supposed to do now?' Lige asked, standing trembling, his arms wrapped around him in the cold, open yard.

'The only thing there is to do,' Carson Banner said, 'ask for shelter.'

The reality of it was that there was very little chance of their being refused. In these far mountains, anywhere across the broad western lands, a man who was hungry was fed if you had food to offer, a man in rough weather taken in for the night. That was just the way things were done, had to be, as each man counted on his neighbors as they could count on him. Still, there was something different about this than approaching a lonesome soddy on the great plains or a miner's shack in the foothills. The house itself did not belong here, and the people who dwelled there were not your ordinary folks.

Still, if Carson could believe what Elijah Tuttle had told him, Sterling March had left his people with instructions to turn no hard-luck traveler away. Perhaps that had something to do with March's memories of his own scuffling days.

'Well, then, knock on the blamed door,' Lige said sourly, 'it's not getting any warmer out here!'

Carson judged that Lige had just about reached the end of his endurance. The wind continued to howl around them and the snow began to fall in earnest as Carson lifted the bronze doorknocker in the shape of a lion's head and banged on the heavy door. It was a minute, maybe two before the door was opened slightly and a white, sunken face peered out at them.

'Who is it?' the old woman asked in an aged, faltering voice. A second voice from behind her boomed:

'Now what!' and the door was flung wide to reveal a wide-shouldered, robust man in his twenties wearing a brown suit and a frown. The old woman cringed away, her lined, sunken face fearful. 'What do you want?' the young man demanded.

'Shelter,' Carson said. Snow was now swirling about his shoulders and against his face.

'Who are you?' the young man asked angrily.

'A passing stranger,' Carson went on. 'I found this man badly wounded and he asked me to bring him over here. I don't know who he is. All he managed to tell me was that his name is Elijah.'

'Lord's sake, Ben,' the tiny woman said, gripping the young man's arm. 'This is Elijah Tuttle from over on the meadows! Don't you recognize him?'

'I haven't seen him but once or twice. All right,' he said heavily, 'you might as well come in.'

'Sakes alive, Ben,' the old woman said in a small, scolding voice. 'You acted as if you were going to turn a needy traveler away from our door, and a neighbor at that! I hate to think what Mr March would say about that!'

'Mr March ain't here,' the young man protested. 'I expect he'd want me to use some discretion about who I let into the house. Besides,' he grumbled, 'we've already had a regular parade of people up here today.'

Elijah groaned and sagged in Carson's arms. Carson looked to the big kid, Ben, for help.

'All right,' Ben said unhappily, 'help me carry him over here.' With a nod of his head he indicated a side corridor with an arched doorway.

'No, sir,' the old woman muttered, 'I don't know what Mr March would have had to say.'

'All right, Mother!' Ben said with irritation, 'I'm taking care of him now. All right?'

'I just don't know . . . ' the old woman's voice trailed off as she disappeared somewhere into the vast interior of the house. Carson had noticed and admired the cavernous house. Everything was of carved, dark wood. An ornate stairway curved up to meet a long gallery where three or four doors were visible. There was a crystal chandelier hanging over the wide front room where two white-brick fireplaces stood. And this, he realized, was only a small part of the huge house. At another time Carson would have taken the time to appreciate the appointments, but now he was worried about getting Lige to bed and about returning to his real reason for being in Sterling March's mansion — finding the missing girls and the stolen money and somehow retrieving both.

The room where they took Lige was impossibly overdecorated with feminine things, ruffles and silks, oil paintings, bric-a-brac and porcelain miniatures. It was as if a woman with no limit to her budget had purchased everything in sight on some glorious shopping spree, which was probably exactly what had happened.

Well, obviously Sterling March was immensely wealthy and not getting any poorer, and Lige had told him that his wife had endured many hard years before they had struck it rich. Maybe it was normal for such women to go overboard — besides, she had needed to decorate fifty rooms.

To Carson it seemed as if there were enough gee-gaws in this one room to adorn an entire house. But then, it wasn't his room, his house or his money being spent.

'Can you get his boots off?' Ben asked.

'I can give it a try.' Carson looked a question at the young man.

'It's just that some of these old mountaineers haven't had a wash-up for months. I had a bad experience once,' the younger man said.

'I'll yank them off,' Carson said, watching the barely opened eyes of the uncomplaining Lige, the bruises and knots on his face. 'Can you get someone to tend his wounds?'

'I'll have Steven or one of the girls look at him,' Ben promised.

'How many people work here exactly?' Carson asked.

'We had a staff of eighteen last month,' Ben said, showing the first hint of a smile now as he watched Carson twist and tug at Lige's left boot. 'Last week one of the maids ran off with our second houseboy, so we're down to sixteen now.'

'Well, good luck to the runaways,' Carson said, pulling Lige's boot free and going to work on the one on his right foot.

'Yes, I wish them well, too. Spending a winter up here can be a brutal experience. We had nine-foot snowdrifts last year. I want to apologize,' he said abruptly, offering a hand to Carson. 'My mother was right. I had no need to act crossly. It's just that things suddenly got a little hectic this afternoon. My name's Ben Howell.'

'Carson Banner,' Carson said, shaking the man's hand, Lige's boot still dangling from the other. 'You were right about one matter, Ben, and if you're sensitive to such things, I'd recommend backing away a little over, even opening the door.'

For Ben Howell had been correct in his assessment. In a situation where hot water was much more than a luxury, but a virtual impossibility, Lige's feet had likely not been bathed in a year.

Lightning crackled, illuminating the room through the sheer-curtained windows, and following thunder rumbled across the mountainside. 'The storm sounds like it means business,' Carson said, arranging Lige's boot against a wall.

'It does, but the really fierce ones are weeks, a month off, I think. That's the usual pattern.' Howell stood frowning down at the battered form of Elijah Tuttle. 'What did you say happened to this man?'

'He didn't tell me,' Carson lied. 'He must have taken a pretty good fall somewhere.'

'I'd say so,' Ben Howell said. He hadn't accepted the lie. Howell had been around enough to know the signs of a serious beating. 'How'd you say you knew old Lige?'

'I never met him before today. He could hardly get off his bed and asked me to bring him over here. I guess he sheltered up here one other winter.'

'I guess he did. I think I remember him, though I was only a boy.'

The two men went out of the room. Carson remained with Ben as they walked the length of a corridor decorated with portraits of unknown men and women.

'What did you mean when you said you'd already had a parade of people up here today?' Carson asked, trying to act as if it were of no real significance to him. Ben waved a hand in a negligent manner.

'Oh, that. We had a party of two men and their women show up at the door.

Said they were on their way to Oregon but had broken a wheel on their wagon. I told them we could have that fixed, but they'd have to wait until the weather cleared a little.'

Carson nodded his disinterest. He had learned all that he could expect to learn. Except . . . They entered a kitchen where three young women stood or sat around gabbing. One of these was a quite-pretty blonde, perched on a butcher's block, her legs swinging. Carson gave her the look she deserved and was rewarded with a warm smile.

'Brenda,' Ben Howell said to one of the older women, 'we've a wounded old man in the King Alfonse room . . . '

'Which one's that? I've only been here ten years.' The other maids tittered. It must have been difficult to find your way around the massive house. It seemed that Mrs Sterling March had decided to give names to each room.

'First one down this hall, room on your left,' Ben said, his expression straight. 'Get Steve Flannigan to help

44

you take a basin and soap down there. Bandages and iodine as well.'

'I think Steve is up in the Queen of Spain room,' the other older maid quipped.

'You know, Martha,' Ben Howell told her, assuming his manager's role, 'no one's making you women stay on here. As a matter of fact at this time of year Mr March is carrying far more employees than he needs to maintain the house . . . '

'Oh, for God's sake, Ben,' Martha said, 'have you gotten too stiff to take a joke? When he was little,' the maid said to the others, 'I used to have to help him button up his pants.'

'Just see that it's done,' Ben said. 'There's a man in pain down there.'

When he turned away, Carson could see that there was a faint smile on his lips. It was apparent to him that the household staff enjoyed gibing with each other.

'Now, about you,' Ben Howell said as they retraced their footsteps down the hallway. 'I suppose you'd like a room close to your friend.'

'As a matter of fact, I'd prefer a room as far away from Lige and everyone else as you can offer.'

Ben paused, lifted an eyebrow and said, 'There's something that you're not telling me.'

'Yes, there is.'

'I suppose that it's none of my business, then,' Ben said, his voice a little tighter now. 'You just wait around here, then. I'll send Daisy along to show you to your room.'

Carson waited near the open doorway to Lige's room, smelling the odor something like three-day-old cooked eggs that emanated from the mountain man's feet as Ben Howell again returned to the kitchen.

Daisy, when she appeared, proved to be the perky little blonde Carson had met but not been introduced to. She approached, hands behind her back with a sort of mincing stride. Carson watched her approach and as he did her cheeks pinkened.

'I've been sent to show you your room,' the girl called Daisy said, looking down at the carpet and scuffing her toe across it.

'Fine,' Carson said, and after a last look in at the sleeping Elijah Tuttle, he asked, 'which way do we go?'

'The visitors wing. Just follow along.'

'Does my room have a name?' Carson asked playfully and got the expected smile from Daisy.

'I suppose it does, but only the Madam knows the names of all of them.'

'What sort of woman is Mrs March?'

'Very nice,' Daisy answered as they crossed the living room and reached the curved staircase. 'She's a little on the nervous side. She fidgets around all the time, rearranging things. Perhaps she needs to be doing something. Me, if I had a house with only three of these rooms, I'd sag down in a chair and never stir again.'

Proceeding along the upstairs corridor hung with still more oil paintings, carpeted in deep blue, Carson noticed that the girl was limping slightly. 'Did you hurt your foot?' he asked.

She glanced at him with wide blue eyes. 'Yes. I was working barefoot in the kitchen — a stupid thing to do, I know, and I broke a glass. I've got a splinter of glass in my foot. Maybe you could take a look at it.'

'I'm not very good at that sort of thing,' Carson told her, not knowing what game the girl was playing, if indeed she was.

The corridor seemed endless; there was only gloom within and at the windows where the settling storm darkened the skies. Sterling March had kept his visitors as far as possible from his own quarters.

'I'd like to have my saddle-bags,' Carson said as they walked on. 'Do you think that man . . . what's his name?'

'Do you mean Jingo?'

'I guess so. We weren't introduced. A small, dark man — he took my horse.'

'That would be Jingo. Yes, I'll have

him carry them over to the house, and I'll bring them up to you.'

Carson nodded his thanks, thinking that the girl was exceptionally accommodating. Maybe there was little for all the servants to do with the owners gone away.

They turned a ninety-degree corner and started down it and Carson found himself face-to-face with the twin dead eyes of a shotgun barrel.

4

It was Lou Weathers who was standing in the hallway looking down the length of a double-barreled shotgun at Carson Banner. Carson had never encountered the man before, but he knew him from his description. Besides, who else could it be in the visitor's wing of the March mansion but one of the thieves he had been following?

'What are you doing?' Daisy shrieked, moving protectively in front of Carson. 'Who do you think you are?'

'I'm sorry, miss, I really am,' Weathers said with false sincerity, lowering the shotgun as his eyes met Carson's, trying to puzzle him out. Weathers could have been forgiven for taking Carson for the maid's boyfriend, the way she had jumped in front of him to shield him.

'What it is,' Weathers explained, 'is that the room they put us in has this

50

gun rack with a lot of beautiful weapons in it. I couldn't resist hefting this scattergun just to get its feel. I couldn't have known someone would be coming around the corner.'

'At the least it was careless of you,' Daisy said hotly. Her breast rose and fell with excitement. Her cheeks were hot. 'It may even be criminal! You have no right touching the master's possessions. And you know that we have rules about carrying guns in this house.'

Lou Weathers' eyes dropped to the belted Colt that Carson wore, but he only said, 'Yes, miss. I'm very sorry.'

'Well ... ' Daisy hesitated, 'just see that it's put back immediately and I won't report it.'

'I'll do that,' Weathers said, shouldering the gun. He wore a small smirk, either at the audacity of the housemaid or at her protectiveness of her assumed boyfriend. What the smirk conveyed to Carson was the inner workings of the outlaw's mind. *If these people only knew who I was ...*

Weathers turned and stalked away down the hall. Daisy turned to face Carson, and looking up, said, 'Doesn't he realize that I could have him thrown out in the storm for breaking house rules?' No. No, he didn't and might not care. Carson marked carefully in his mind the room into which Weathers vanished. He had to find the women, preferably Ruth Prince alone, and see if they were willing to be returned to the Nine-Slash-Seven after this excursion into the winter high country and a few days in the company of Bill Saxon and Weathers.

If they were not willing, they and the money would have to somehow be taken.

The thing that worried Carson was that the women now settled out of the storm in the March mansion's comforts might begin to lose the memory of the hardships of the long trail. He could see Candice, in her present situation, thinking that the trip would be just a few days of trial with comfort at the end until their trail reached Oregon. Ruth, being older, would not be susceptible to a young girl's imaginings as to how the world worked — or would she?

Carson had never met either one of them; he had only Julian Prince's word as to their characters. Prince had described Ruth as level-headed, practical and unusually protective of her younger sister. Carson could only hope that at least a part of that was true.

'Here we are,' Daisy said, swinging open the door to a room only slightly less opulent than the rest of the house. Carved dark wood, heavy blue velvet drapes, thick blue carpet.

'No wonder people choose this place to be snowbound,' he said, sitting on the four-poster bed with its lemon-yellow bedspread. Daisy made herself at home, sitting at the gilt chair near the white, claw-footed dresser. She was unlacing one of her tiny boots.

'Are you going to look at my foot now?' she asked with a childlike smile.

'I suppose I should,' he answered,

'seeing as you saved my life at your own peril.'

'Oh, that,' Daisy said, waving a hand dismissively. 'That man was just fooling around. He didn't mean us any harm.'

Not you, Carson was thinking, but if Lou Weathers had had any idea who Carson Banner was it might have been a different story.

Daisy's bare foot had found its way to Carson's lap. He examined it briefly.

'I might need a needle,' Carson told Daisy, 'and I haven't got one.'

'That's no problem,' Daisy said, turning up the hem of her black skirt. She extracted a sewing needle from among a group of pins. She held it up before offering it to Carson. 'A ladies' maid always has to be ready to sew a button or mend a rip.'

'Very handy,' Carson said, turning the foot a little more toward the light. As he bent to examine it, he said. 'That man in the hall wasn't very pleasant, was he?'

'No, but you are,' Daisy said,

becoming coquettish.

'Thank you,' he answered. Carson had found the nearly invisible glass splinter and he began probing the pad of Daisy's heel with the needle. She winced and smiled at once.

Carson said, 'I guess you'll be taking care of the women who arrived with them.'

'If they need something. Mostly Brenda and I will just check on the room when they're out, dusting and pulling the beds together. Any heavier work is taken care of by some of the other girls.'

'I see — and when are they usually out of their room? For dinner, I assume.'

'That's right. For all of their meals,' Daisy told him, wincing again as the needle dug deeper. 'It gives us plenty of time to whisk in and whisk out, changing towels and such.'

'I see.' Carson asked her, 'Is there any chance of me whisking in and out while they're down at the dinner table?'

'Of course not! Why would you ask such a question? If you were caught you'd be evicted, and if I were caught letting you in, I'd likely be sacked.'

'I just thought I'd ask,' Carson said. He thought if he could poke around a little while the woman were out, he might find Julian Prince's stolen money. It was more likely that the men, Saxon and Weathers, had it, but you never knew.

'Well, you shouldn't have asked a question like that,' Daisy scolded. 'It makes you sound like a thief or something.'

'You're right,' Carson said, digging a little deeper than was necessary to extract the glass splinter and hold it up to the light for Daisy to see. She was not smiling now; neither was he. Well, maybe that would be enough to cool Daisy down. If she was not going to be his ally, he did not need her hanging around as a hindrance.

'That's it,' Carson said, returning the needle.

'Yes. Thank you,' Daisy said a little stiffly. He had managed to dampen her mood. He walked to the window as she put her stocking and shoe back on. When she left the room without another word, he stood staring down at the storm. All was gray-white beyond the window with the exception of a few stark black oak trees with barren, projecting arms. The snow fell in blue-white flurries. When it touched the ground the wind immediately formed it into serpentine ridges. It would be drifting against the walls of the huge house soon. Ben Howell had mentioned having nine-foot drifts stacked against it one year.

Carson couldn't sit around and wait to see if this winter was going to be as bad — or worse. He had a job to do and it couldn't be done as long as his prey was holed up comfortably in the house where all was comfort and warmth. There had to be a way to pry them free of it, but he had no idea what it was. He could not spend a winter snowbound in the mountains. He should at least look in on Lige again — assuming he could find his way to the mountain man's room without a map or guide.

'Didn't you hear the dinner gong?' Ben Howell asked from the open doorway.

'No, I guess I didn't,' Carson answered although it seemed there had been some barely registering chime-like sound while he stood meditating at the window.

'Louis might not have turned this way. He wouldn't have known there was anyone in this wing. Anyway,' Ben said with a smile, 'we've got the table set for dinner if you want to follow along.'

'Happy to,' Carson said, starting that way. Ben Howell met him with a frown and a shake of his head.

'You can't be wearing that belt gun around this house, Carson. Sorry, but those are the rules.'

'All right,' Carson said, shedding his gun and tossing it on to the bed. He wasn't happy with the edict, but he understood it.

'No one else will be wearing one either,' Howell said. 'Sterling March's orders — or rather Mrs March's — they want this house to be a patch of civilization on the wild country.'

'All right,' Carson said. 'Can't have house guests shooting each other.'

'We have had — in the old days — that's the reason for the rule. A couple of roaming men brought their outside trouble inside. Nearly drove Mrs March into a conniption fit when they started shooting at each other. Sterling laid down firm rules after that.' He paused as they went out into the corridor. Striding along the carpeted hallway, Ben Howell asked, 'You haven't brought any outside troubles in with you, have you, Carson?'

'Me? Why do you ask?'

'Carson, maybe I'm none too clever, but when it comes to what's going on in this house, I'm observant — that's what Sterling March pays me for. Elijah — I don't know what happened to him, but it looks to me like he was beaten with fists. This is a sparsely settled land, Carson; there just aren't that many people living around here, and I can't see why any of them would have a reason to beat Elijah Tuttle.

'Shortly after that must have happened we had a group of strangers show up here — and you know how remote this house is. I don't like it. My instinct is to toss the bunch of you out,' Ben Howell said, shaking his head as they started down the long, curved staircase. 'Something stinks around here, and it's not Elijah's feet.'

It sure wasn't dinner. Carson sat to the table and went at his meal which consisted of ham, corn on the cob, glazed yams with raisins and walnuts, mashed potatoes with red-eye gravy followed by coffee and chocolate éclairs.

Carson enjoyed the meal, but he spent much of his time observing his fellow diners.

The brutish Lou Weathers he had already met upstairs. Bill Saxon was something of a surprise. The man was blond, fresh-faced, his wavy hair brushed straight back from his high forehead. The man of Candice Prince's teenage dreams.

The women were much as he had pictured them, except both were prettier. They had apparently had the help of the housemaids with their dresses and hair. Ruth Prince sat erectly, never at a loss as to which spoon or fork to use. What might have been a diamond brooch sparkled on the front of her caramel-colored dress. She seldom entered the conversation, but sat watching each of the men with apparent disapproval. Ruth was still young, but she had the mannerisms of a matron.

Candice Prince acted like her sixteen-year-old self. Wearing a yellow dress with white ruffles at the neck and cuffs, she alternately fidgeted, poked broodingly at her food and broke into girlish laughter, frequently leaning closer to Bill Saxon to whisper something or other which Saxon usually ignored.

Neither of the women seemed especially perturbed by their present situation.

Ben Howell, who had just returned, sat at the head of the table as the others finished eating.

'What about our wagon?' Lou Weathers demanded, not wasting time on any pleasantries.

'We'll see to it in the morning, if the storm lets up,' Ben responded. His expression said that he was not fond of the bull-necked, surly Weathers. 'Jingo can find a wheel that will fit among our supply. I'll send him and ... ' Ben hesitated, trying to decide who to send along.

'I'll go,' Carson spoke up. He was leaning away from the table, thumbs hooked into his belt.

'You're a guest,' Ben Howell said.

'I've eaten your food; I'll do some work to repay you,' Carson said easily. 'It beats sitting around the house.'

Lou Weathers was glowering at Carson; it was obvious that he did not like the idea of Carson going along. Bill Saxon looked thoughtfully at the white napkin he was folding, saying nothing.

'All right,' Ben said, 'if we get a break in the weather tomorrow morning, I'll tell Jingo to have a spare wheel and tools loaded on the buckboard. It shouldn't take long to get you folks rolling again.' He added this last almost hopefully. They were leaving, weren't they?

'Should we really be traveling in this weather?' Ruth Prince asked Bill Saxon.

He smiled and replied. 'You wouldn't want to be stuck here all winter, would you?'

'No, I suppose not,' Ruth answered a little regretfully. 'Tell whoever baked those éclairs that they were delicious, won't you, Mr Howell.'

'That was my mother — yes. I'll be sure to tell her.'

The others rose to take a short walking tour of the house, guided by Daisy, who deliberately avoided looking at Carson. Howell told Carson as they stepped aside, 'That's one of the requirements for guests. Taking a tour of the house. Mrs March wants all of its grandness shown off.' He did not, however, try to talk Carson into joining the others.

'I guess I'd better look in on Lige before turning in. Have you seen him?' Carson asked.

'A while ago,' Ben said, walking that way with Carson. 'He was resting comfortably, though with his face all bandaged and bruised he still looks like hell.'

'As long as he is resting . . . and safe,' Carson replied.

'Is there any reason that he shouldn't be safe?' Ben Howell asked.

'Probably not,' Carson said. 'Let's just say that, like you, my nose is twitching a little bit.'

'I see,' Howell said as they crossed the living room toward the corridor where Elijah Tuttle had his room. 'You're still not going to tell me about it, are you?'

'No. Let's put it this way, Ben, it has

nothing to do with you or the house, and I'd think you'd want to keep it that way.'

Tuttle, propped up in bed on a few pillows, was sipping thick soup from a bowl held by another of the house-maids, a redhead Carson had not seen before. The mountain man's eyes flickered toward the doorway as they entered and he smiled almost shyly.

'How are you doing, Lige?'

'Me? I somehow made my way to heaven!' Elijah replied. The old man's chest was bound tightly; he wore a cap of white bandages; the area around one eye was swollen, bruised to yellow and purple, but he was smiling through split lips.

'All right, just wanted to check up on you,' Carson told him.

'I'm doing fine. Thank you, Carson. And thank you, Mr Howell — you're a man who sure knows how to treat his guests.'

Ben Howell nodded his head and both men eased back out the door.

'He's doing well enough without us,' Ben said as they walked away. 'Virginia's taken him in hand.'

'She'll spoil him,' Carson agreed. 'The man's not used to that kind of attention.'

They said goodbye at the foot of the stairs and Carson made his way up toward his room. He did not think Saxon and Lou Weathers would make a move to escape on this stormy night. They needed to have their wagon repaired before hitting the long trail again — if that could be done at all in this weather. Still, Carson meant to leave his door open and sleep lightly.

Those two were plain no good and there was no telling what sort of mischief they might get up to.

After blowing out his lantern, Carson slipped into bed and lay listening to the whistle and bluster of the storm outside. He wondered as he lay awake — where was the other man on this terrible night?

For he had not forgotten about

young Wesley Short, who had ridden away from his job at the Julian Prince's Nine-Slash-Seven ranch in pursuit of Candice. Where had the kid from the 9/7 gotten to? If Saxon and Weathers had not already taken care of him somewhere along the trail, then he was out in the blizzard, perhaps sheltering up in a cave. Or maybe he had moved into Lige's cabin to wait out the weather. That would have been his best move.

Despite his own earlier speculation, it was obvious that the young Wesley Short had no connection with Weathers and Bill Saxon. His only wish was to take Candice Prince home to the Nine-Slash-Seven.

How? It seemed that blind impulse had set Short on their trail; the kid probably had no plan at all besides hope. That he had stuck to their trail for this long did prove that he was serious in his intention to rescue Candice from the thieves.

But then, Carson knew where good

intentions could lead an ill-equipped man . . .

The sound came again — from within the house and not without. It was the creak of a floorboard in the carpeted hallway. Someone was out and moving around in the dark of night.

5

Carson Banner was on his feet in seconds, one easy glide from the bed. His first impulse was to grab for his Colt revolver, but remembering his circumstances he left it where it was and slipped out into the hallway, which was black as sin. Beyond the walls the storm raged — there was no helpful moonlight. He paused where he was and listened. Again he heard movement down along the hallway which led to the curved staircase.

Who, and why? He could not guess, but there were thieves about in the March house on this night. Rather, a single one, for there was only one man ahead of him, moving stealthily along the corridor — or as stealthily as a heavy, clumsy man could manage. A lighter man such as Bill Saxon could not have caused the vibration that Carson felt in the floor with his stockinged feet. It was Lou Weathers beyond any doubt; the man defied all those stories about light-footed big men. He was the plodding sort.

Carson eased down the hallway behind him, still wondering where Weathers could be going at this time of night. Maybe that evening's tour of the mansion had shown him some valuable piece that he coveted. More likely, he meant to administer another beating to Lige Tuttle as he had promised the old man.

Carson could not allow either occurrence.

His host and hostess must not be robbed; Lige must be protected.

Carson could think of no innocent reason for Lou Weathers to be out and about at this hour. The rooms all contained those marvelous and expensive new indoor bathrooms; he could not be slipping down for a midnight snack. It was doubtful he could even find the kitchen in the dark, in this house. Carson doubted that he himself could.

Lou Weathers — for there was no doubt now that that was who the man was — continued on toward the top of the curved staircase. From below the last glow of a dying fire in one of the massive white-brick fireplaces still dully illuminated the living room, and Weathers' bulky form was visible by its light. He carried no obvious weapon, and that was for the better.

But neither was Carson Banner armed, and if it came to a face-to-face fight, Carson was not confident of his ability to take care of the man. Lou Weathers had at least fifty pounds more weight on him. Nevertheless, he could not be let alone to go about his business no matter what it might be.

'Get lost?' Carson said, slipping up beside Lou Weathers as he hesitated at the top of the stairs, peering down into the living room. 'It's easy to do; I guess that's why they don't like guests roaming around out here.'

'Who in hell are you?' Weathers said, turning bearish black eyes, which glittered in the faint light of the fire coals, on Carson. Carson Banner held up a hand.

'Just a fellow traveler,' he said in what he hoped was a conciliatory tone.

'Travel on in some other direction,' Weathers said, 'before you start to annoy me.'

'Annoy you?' Carson said innocently. 'Why, we're all here to help each other. That's why I mean to help you repair your wagon in the morning.' He shook his head. 'But Ben Howell told me that they don't like people wandering around the mansion. I thought I'd tell you in case you hadn't gotten the word.'

'To hell with Ben Howell,' Weathers said from out of the darkness, 'and to hell with you, too. I'm a man who goes where he feels like going and no one tells me otherwise.'

'That can be an unhealthy habit,' Carson said in a different voice, one that was not quite so innocent.

'It's like that, is it?' Weathers growled. 'I don't know who you are, friend, but I almost regret that that shotgun I was holding earlier wasn't loaded. And now you don't even have your little girl-friend to help you out.'

'Oh, I don't think I need her,' Carson said in a voice that was soft but somehow taunting. 'You don't look half so big without a gun in your hands.'

'You have no idea who I am, do you?' Lou Weathers said, his voice rising.

'Besides being a cheap thief and a bully — no, I don't,' Carson said, knowing instantly that he had gone too far.

Lou Weathers was not slow in reacting — immediate response to any implied challenge was his way. Weathers threw a meaty fist at Carson's skull, but Carson, expecting it, beat him to it with a sharp kick at Weathers' knee. Even without his boot, the impact of the kick was solid and disabling.

Weathers turned half-away in baffled pain and Carson was able to drive his fist down against the base of Lou's skull, stunning the big man so that he lost his balance and tumbled noisily down the curved staircase in front of him.

The thudding of his body falling brought the lower house to life. Lamps were lit in half a dozen rooms and men came forward carrying lanterns, Ben Howell leading the way wearing a nightshirt and hastily drawn-up trousers.

'What's going on here?' Howell demanded, holding his lantern high as he passed the sprawled figure of Lou Weathers, who was struggling to pull himself upright.

'Beats me — he must have fallen in the darkness. I heard it myself just now and rushed along to help.'

Ben Howell glared unhappily at Carson, the lantern light flickering across his face. 'I didn't think you'd lie to me, Carson.'

'Lie? I don't know what you mean.' Behind Carson the two women had reached them — Ruth and Candice Prince along with a robed Bill Saxon, who seemed not a bit concerned about his friend.

'How is he?' Ruth asked, clutching her green robe together at the throat.

74

'He'll be all right,' one of the men below them on the staircase — Steve Flannigan? — answered, 'he's just a little dazed.'

'Good,' Ben said. 'A couple of you boys get him up and help him to his room. The rest of you — get back to bed and stay there for the night!' The women swept away followed by an apparently indifferent Bill Saxon, who spared only a single closely examining glance for Carson Banner.

Carson had also turned to go but Ben Howell caught him by the elbow. 'Just a minute, Carson, I never did finish my story.'

'Your story?' Carson said blankly.

'The one about the two old-timers who started a shooting affair in this house, frightening Mrs March out of her wits.'

'Yes, you said that Sterling March laid down the law after that.'

'You've never met Sterling March,' Ben said as he accompanied Carson down the hallway, carrying his lantern.

'Now he's a most respectable brewery owner, but for many years he roved the rough gold camps struggling to make his first fortune. It wasn't an easy time or place.

'When these two yahoos came in here upsetting his wife he laid down the law, all right — with his big old Colt Walker revolver. He sent us out to bury them in the morning — want me to show you the spot?'

'That doesn't seem necessary,' Carson said as they rounded the corner of the corridor toward his room.

'No, I guess it's not,' Ben said as they paused at the door. 'I just wanted to let you know that I still keep that Walker on my bedside table.'

'I'll keep that in mind,' Carson answered. Then with a final nod to Ben Howell, he went into his bedroom, relit the lantern and began to pull off his shirt.

He had not closed the door tightly and the woman in the green dressing gown slipped into his room. Ruth

Prince's dark hair was down around her shoulders, her feet bare. An almost smile, an inquisitive look played across her lips. She was even younger than Carson had guessed — Candice's 'big sister' could not have been more than twenty years old.

'Is there something I can do for you?' Carson asked, rising from the bed. Ruth watched as he folded his blue shirt and placed it on top of the dressing table. Her look said that he had folded it all wrong and she could show him the proper way.

After a moment's silence as Carson stood bare-chested before her, she managed to say, 'I hope there is something that you can do for us. I don't know who you are, but let me ask you this — have you ever spoken to my father, Julian Prince?'

'I'm not sure I should tell you,' Carson answered.

'That means 'yes', I assume. We do need some help, but your answer indicates that you don't know if you can

77

trust me or not.'

'Does it?' Carson shrugged. 'If you say so.'

'You know that you missed an opportunity, don't you?' Ruth asked. 'You should have just finished Lou Weathers off while you had the chance.'

'Not the proper time or place,' Carson answered. 'Besides, I'm hoping it doesn't come to that — with either of them.'

'Are we really traveling on in the morning — if the wagon is repairable?'

'That's the way I understand the plan.' Carson decided to ask her flat-out. 'Ruth, where is the stolen money?'

Before she could answer there was the faintest tap at the door and the slender figure of Daisy appeared in the doorway, clutching Carson's heavy saddle-bags with both hands. Her eyes opened wide at the sight of Ruth Prince and then squinted nearly shut as she thrust the saddle-bags toward Carson.

'I told you that I'd bring these to you,' Daisy said, using a tone like that of an injured wife.

'Thanks,' was all Carson had time to mutter before Daisy spun away and went out, her small feet making large noises against the carpeted floor. There was a faint smile on Ruth Prince's mouth.

'Your girlfriend?'

'No,' Carson answered, dropping the saddle-bags beside the bed. 'Just a lonely girl suffering from a common affliction — she's very young.'

Ruth sighed and stretched. 'I'm familiar with that affliction,' she replied. 'It seems to be going around the mountains just now.'

'It does, doesn't it?'

Ruth turned toward the door without having answered Carson's question about the stolen money. Perhaps she did not wish to. She had no real reason to trust Carson Banner — that could have been it. Or perhaps Ruth Prince had her own plans for the money. That was not a comforting thought, but it would explain why she wished for Carson to get rid of their two rough escorts.

There was no point in examining the woman's motives. He did not know her nor her thoughts. Carson slipped back into bed and rolled up comfortably, listening to the muted sounds of the raging storm outside.

No sound awakened Carson Banner in the morning. It was the absence of sound that stirred some inner instinct to rise to his feet in the dull glow of predawn light.

The storm had blown itself out. The sky outside was clear for the most part, fogged by thin, sketchy clouds which had just begun to color in the minutes before sunrise. Carson Banner was eager to be going. He could not foretell what this morning held, but he knew that he would be moving forward with the larger plan which included returning the stolen money and Julian Prince's daughters to the Nine-Slash-Seven if it could be done.

He was still a lone man against two desperate thieves and one — or both? — of Prince's fractious daughters. He was not sure of Ruth's loyalties, but it was clear that Candice Prince would wish to follow her dream to its end even if that meant sealing her own fate. Sixteen-year-olds can seldom see past today into the complications of tomorrow. Certainly Carson, himself, had been that way. He could only shake his head at some of the reckless decisions he had made in his life.

Dressed now as the sun began to brighten the window to his room, he slipped out after first fastening his gun belt. He made his way downstairs, seeing no one. He was hungry, but did not intend to wait around for breakfast.

Carson Banner had traveling on his mind.

The deepest of the snow was only ankle high on his boots as he rounded the corner of the big house, the cold wind gusting against his back, in the dawn light of the new morning, his saddle-bags over his shoulder.

The dark little man darted out to meet Carson. 'I get 'im,' Jingo said eagerly, his eyes bright with willingness. 'You wanna ride 'im away today, I get your fine horse for you.'

'Thanks, Jingo,' Carson said, with some difficulty falling into stride with the scuttling hostler. 'Did you find a Conestoga wheel for the others?'

'I have a fine wheel I found in our place to take the ladies away. Got some fine tools along to do the job real shortly.'

Jingo continued to smile. Everything in his world seemed to be fine. In a distant way Carson envied Jingo's cheerfulness. Everything in Carson's own world was not fine, might not be for a long while to come. There must be a story behind how the Indian had come to work at the March house, but there was no time to go into it with the little man. There may have been a lot of sadness behind it. And what of a young girl like Daisy . . . ?

Carson deliberately broke off that thought. The less he considered the blonde girl, the better. He didn't need that sort of complication in his life, though he wished he had taken the time to try to explain things a little more to her.

The barn had a massive interior. A loft ran along its entire length, shading fifty horse stalls. Carson could only imagine how much money it cost Sterling March to build it, to keep it provided with forage for fifty horses. There were only nine or ten animals housed there at the present — that Carson could see — the four-horse wagon team among them. Along its great length there could be any number of animals that weren't evident and which he needed to know nothing about. He did once hear the braying of a mule — Jingo's stolen Sally, he supposed.

Jingo led him to where his curiously marked gray horse stood, whiskers of hay at the corners of its mouth.

''Im is a fine horse,' Jingo said, stroking the gray's muzzle.

'Yes, he is,' Carson agreed. Then

more roughly, 'Though what he's good for, I don't know.'

'Oh, you know, boss,' the smiling Jingo said, ''im is good at getting you from here to there.'

'I suppose you're right,' Carson had to agree, smiling himself now. 'Jingo, did you put some sort of long lever in the buckboard? We'll have to raise the wagon somehow.'

'Sure, boss,' Jingo said as he hefted Carson's saddle. 'Good long piece of timber. We pick him up real easy. Got blocks to hold 'im up; even some grease for the new wheel.' Jingo grinned. 'I do this plenty of times. Always people come up here breaking wheels, even axles. We fix 'im good.'

Which was just what they needed to do; for everyone's sake it was best to get that wagon moving, even though Carson had a different idea on what direction it should be traveling than Saxon and Lou Weathers.

Carson took a minute to ask Jingo if he had seen a young, fair-haired man around, maybe stealing some sleep in the barn, but Jingo had not seen anything of Wesley Short. Where had the kid gotten to? It would be nice to know.

Carson Banner waited on the tailgate of the buckboard after briefly checking its load. The sun floated higher, bleaching out the snowscape covering the mountains. Jingo rolled a cigarette for himself and had finished smoking it down before the travelers appeared.

Ben Howell was escorting the small party, looking none too happy on this morning. The two women wore fur-collared, nearly identical brown coats with Candice's a shade lighter than her sister's. Neither woman bothered to greet Carson or seemed to wish to meet his eyes.

Bill Saxon strode across the snowy yard, erect in a gray suit, hat and over-coat, trying apparently to make himself appear the gentlemanly figure he considered himself to be. Lou Weathers, in a sheepskin-lined leather jacket, swaggered beside him, looking like the barroom bully that he was. Both of the men glanced at Carson. Bill Saxon's glance was quick, furtive; Lou Weathers' was challenging, dark with venom.

Carson Banner slipped from the buckboard's tailgate to meet Ben Howell.

'I guess this is so-long, Ben. I'd like to thank you for putting up with us.'

'It wasn't my choice,' Ben reminded him. 'Mother put her foot down.'

Carson smiled. Ben was continuing on toward the horse barn. 'Going somewhere?' Carson asked.

'With you, of course,' Ben Howell responded. 'I won't be satisfied until I see that wagon repaired and back on the road.'

Carson nodded, saying nothing. He retrieved his gray horse as Ben, accompanied by the always-animated Jingo, led a buckskin horse out of a stall to be saddled. 'Two more,' he heard Ben tell the stableman. 'It doesn't matter which ones; they won't be going far.'

Ben glanced at Carson Banner and said almost defensively, 'Well we can't have them all riding crammed together on the buckboard seat,' although Carson had made no comment.

Ben Howell was still playing host, albeit a reluctant one. It was more than obvious that Ben just wanted them all gone from his own little winter kingdom. Elijah, of course, would remain. The ill and wounded were not turned out of the big house, and Elijah Tuttle additionally was a local man, more to be trusted.

None of that was a concern to Carson. He fiddled with his saddle-bags and cinch straps, eyeing Saxon and Weathers. Neither man was wearing a visible gun, which did not necessarily mean that they were unarmed. Lou Weathers, especially, Carson did not think would be walking around without iron.

Bill Saxon was in close conversation with the pert little Candice Prince. He looked embarrassed, weary of her as he usually did when talking to the eager young girl. Did Candice even notice it? Ruth obviously did, but she turned her back deliberately; it was difficult to guess what was going on in Ruth's mind. It was not so difficult to tell what was going on in the dark mind of Lou Weathers as he leaned against the buckboard's front wheel and leered at Ruth. He was just waiting for his chance, and he was sure that it would come.

Bill Saxon seemed uncomfortable with the present situation, and Carson was having trouble figuring the smooth little con man out. He was in it for the money, obviously, but watching him around Candice Prince gave Carson pause to wonder if Saxon wasn't considering that the price might be a little too high. Candice was young, attractive, nicely formed, but her manner seemed to irritate the older, presumably more experienced Bill Saxon.

'Straddle your ponies, men,' Ben Howell called out in a manner reminiscent of a trail boss beginning a cattle drive as the four-horse wagon team was led out of the barn and tethered to the rear of the buckboard. He himself was already on the back of the buckskin chosen from the group in the horse barn, Carson sat in leather on his gray. The two thieves, Saxon and Weathers, mounted two similar red roan horses provided for them. The eager Jingo scampered toward the buckboard as the two Prince sisters stepped up without assistance, skirts and coats hoisted, and settled on to the spring seat. Candice turned her head to look for Bill Saxon; Ruth kept her dark eyes fixed straight ahead.

They trailed slowly forth in the chill of morning. The skies were still mostly uncluttered with storm clouds. A few ragged, morning-colored banners drifted among the mountain peaks. The forest was still, long and white. They had a fine day to work with; what tomorrow might bring was anyone's guess.

6

The road they traveled seemed vaguely familiar to Carson; it seemed to parallel the route he had ridden on his way to the March house.

They crossed a hummocked snow-field, passing through the dark shadows of the giant pines, and found the broken wagon lying below them in the shallow gully. The wind had picked up and Carson had to strain to hear Ben Howell as he yelled something to Jingo.

' . . . that's the job. Can you take care of it!'

'I fix 'im, boss. I fix 'im real good. In no time,' the smiling little man answered.

'Yes,' Howell muttered, 'see that you do. Tie our horses on behind and bring them home with you, do you hear me?'

'Sure, I hear you, boss,' Jingo answered.

Turning his horse, Ben Howell rode to the other side of the buckboard where its uncertain passengers waited. The wind ruffled the fur on the hoods of the women's coats.

'Well, here you are,' Carson heard Ben Howell say. 'Jingo knows what he's doing. He'll get you rolling again. Goodbye and good luck.'

The women's expressions indicated that they were surprised that Howell was pulling out; Carson was not a bit surprised. They had been unwelcome guests in the first place. Now, clear of Sterling March's property, they were on their own. Really, Carson thought fairly, there was little more that Howell could have done, and nothing more they should have expected.

Jingo started the buckboard down the slope, Bill Saxon and Lou Weathers following. Carson held back for a minute. Ben was making his way back toward the house through the snow, not so much as glancing back. Carson kneed his pony and started along after the others. He knew he was going to have to offer some sort of explanation for remaining behind with them. For now his reason was simply that he was willing to work. Neither Bill Saxon nor Lou Weathers had made a move toward the rear of the wagon to assist Jingo with his job, and it was not a one-man task.

The long lever Jingo had brought was positioned under the bed of the wagon, which, Carson remembered, still held several heavy items, a flour barrel included. Jingo had unloaded the Conestoga wheel from the buckboard and rolled it through the snow to the rear axle. Jingo let it fall and looked to Carson to hoist the rear of the wagon — if he could — while Jingo unfastened the broken wheel with the tools he had brought along. The hub key was very tight, Carson could tell as Jingo strained at the lock.

Men were very careless about maintaining their rolling stock. The slightest nick on a horse's flesh might be tended immediately, but ranchers seemed to begrudge the use of a few drops of oil

— maybe a part of that was the cowhand's well-known disinclination to do any job that could not be done from horseback.

The rusted axle nut came free with a loud snap and Jingo looked up, grinning. Then the real work was going to begin — for both of them. Jingo was going to try to remove the broken wheel and replace it after Carson had levered the wagon upward. Jingo would use block after block of wood to elevate the wagon, hoping it did not slip away — and since they were on uneven ground, there was that chance.

Candice and Ruth Prince sat on the buck-board's seat, watching and chatting. Bill Saxon stared at the proceedings — a disinterested spectator — from horseback as Lou Weathers wandered about idly, kicking at the snow or cursing in a muffled voice. Neither man lifted a finger to help as Carson labored on, lifting the wagon higher, and Jingo scuttled around the bed of the Conestoga trying to position blocks which always seemed to be an inch too large. The long wooden pole was digging quite painfully into Carson's shoulder before Jingo finally waved and frantically indicated that the axle had been raised enough for changing the wheel.

Jingo positioned the new wheel as Carson stood catching his breath, the lever across his shoulder. The little man's face now wore a concerned look.

'What's the matter, Jingo?'

''Im not too good, boss.'

'What do you mean? What's the trouble?'

'Axle pin — 'im's all splintered like nobody's business, boss.'

'What's this? What's going on?' Bill Saxon demanded, striding up to where Jingo crouched over the wheel.

'Broken axle shaft,' Carson said in quick explanation. 'You can see where it splintered off when the wheel gave way.'

'Yes, but what's that mean? Can't we travel on?'

Both Prince sisters heard that and they were stirred to alertness.

'Jingo?' Carson asked, knowing that the little man had more experience with these problems than any of them.

' 'Im go a little far, but not too far,' the dark man said. 'Maybe to a town that can fix 'im.'

'Not to Oregon?' Candice asked the obviously childish question.

'No, 'im not go to Oregon,' Jingo said with a sad little shake of his head. 'Maybe you have good luck, you go maybe a hundred miles. You go to town, get 'im fixed.'

'What town?' Bill Saxon asked unhappily, looking out across the long mountains.

'Maybe it could be repaired back at the March place,' Ruth suggested. Jingo squelched that idea.

'Boss, him tell me no bring you back to the big house. You have to go, go to Tumble Oaks. Good luck and you make 'im.'

'What's that?' Candice asked, touching her breast with her fingertips as if someone had told them to go to Hades.

'I've heard of the town,' Lou Weathers said. 'It's just a little blood-and-whiskey hole down along the river,' he said, lifting his chin toward the bottom land to indicate the settlement.

'It sounds fearsome,' Ruth Prince said.

'You got nothing to worry about,' Lou Weathers told her, 'not as long as I'm with you.' The comment did nothing to calm Ruth's concerns. She obviously was not happy with Weathers in the role of her protector.

'Surely there's another place around where we can have the axle fixed,' Bill Saxon said to Jingo. Candice now clung to his arm, looking up at his face fearfully. Jingo could only shrug and answer:

'Maybe in Oregon is a lot of places. You can't make it there. Here only got one place. You go to Tumble Oaks, there is a good man to do 'im.'

'Tumble Oaks it is,' Bill Saxon said with a heavy sigh as he stood looking down the long mountain slopes. Lou

Weathers started to say something, but Saxon cut him off. 'There's no other choice, Lou.'

'I suppose not,' Weathers said, walking away through the snow toward his borrowed horse.

'Them ponies,' Jingo said, 'they don't go to Tumble Oaks. Them Boss March's fine ponies. I tie them on behind my buckboard and take them home.'

'What do you mean?' Bill Saxon asked Jingo, who was busy mounting the new wheel on the damaged axle. 'We need those horses.' Jingo shook his head stubbornly.

''Im Boss March's horses. Boss Howell, he says bring 'im home. You got here with no horses, you can get going without 'im.'

Carson smiled even though there was really nothing amusing about the situation. What they had was a pair of accomplished thieves who were being given a chance to travel on out of charity yet thought they had the right to take Sterling March's horses.

'What about you?' Ruth asked Carson unexpectedly. 'Which way are you riding?'

'Why, there's no other road — I'm going to Tumble Oaks with you.'

Ruth Prince's expression seemed to reflect gratitude. That of Lou Weathers definitely did not.

'Nobody's invited you, cowboy.'

'That's all right. I'll just be traveling along in the same direction — I'll keep you in sight in case you get into trouble again.'

'You are the trouble,' Lou Weathers growled.

'Oh, you're starting to realize that now, are you?' With that and a smile, Carson stepped into his stirrup and swung aboard the gray horse. Weathers muttered something which might have been a pointless curse or a threat. It didn't matter which to Carson Banner.

He rode directly toward the treeline, pausing only after entering the forest to look back and watch the four travelers beginning their trek again. Jingo could still be seen, driving the buckboard steadily homeward, the two saddled roan horses tethered behind. By the time he had disappeared from sight, Lou Weathers had started the heavy wagon down the mountain toward the distant, hidden town of Tumble Oaks, making slow going of it through the snow.

What Carson had told them was true — he could watch them, follow along well enough from a distance. There was no point in reminding the abrasive Weathers that he was still with them. What Carson needed, he was beginning to realize, was help. He would have liked to be convinced that Ruth Prince was on his side — or could be persuaded to come over to it. Surely she knew who had the stolen money. Unless she coveted it herself . . . Carson knew nothing about either woman except for what he had been told by their father and the little or next to nothing he had been able to gather from observing them. Maybe Ruth was not as content on the Nine-Slash-Seven as her father believed and would welcome the opportunity of moving to new country every bit as much as her younger sister — especially if she had hopes, plans to keep the money for herself.

Carson could not make any judgments at this time. All he knew at this point was that the bad blood between himself and Lou Weathers would come to a boil before things could be settled.

Carson Banner would let the travelers go as far as Tumble Oaks, but he could not allow them to travel farther on into the winter wilderness. The deeper into the mountains they went, the more difficult the job would become.

Things would have to be settled there one way or the other.

He let the gray find its own way along the flank of the snow-frosted mountain slope, winding slowly through the deep-blue, snow-draped pines.

He had come to a mountain valley and was beginning to cross it when the voice of the man in the trees barked out:

'Hold up right there, mister!'

Carson immediately flung his left hand high although he held the reins in his right, not far from the butt of his holstered Colt. He had had occasion to fake surrender in that manner before. Usually it was accepted, as it was now.

The gray horse stood blowing steam from its nostrils into the cold air. Carson did not move, but from the corner of his eye he could see another rider, mounted on a shaggy dun horse, riding out to meet him. The rider held a Winchester rifle loosely in one hand.

The voice which had hailed him was now softer. 'I had to stop you,' the man said. 'You would have ridden right into them.'

Carson turned his head slightly to study the younger blond man. 'Wesley Short?' he asked.

'That's right,' the kid answered. 'How'd you know?'

'I've been wondering where you'd gotten to.'

The former Nine-Slash-Seven rider

looked puzzled. 'How did you even know I existed?' he asked Carson.

'Something was said back at the ranch. I'm working for Mr Prince. Who were you trying to warn me about?'

'There they come now,' Wesley Short said, lifting a gloved, pointing finger, and squinting that way Carson could see two mounted men emerging from the forest to the east, crossing the valley.

Wesley must have seen the frown on Carson's face, because before Carson could ask him a question, Wesley Short said, 'You didn't think they were alone, did you — Saxon and Lou Weathers?'

'I'd been hoping so,' Carson replied. 'I never saw anyone else.'

'They were off following my trail,' Wesley said. 'They lost my tracks when the snow fell. I holed up in some old trapper's cabin and let the storm drift by, though I was afraid of losing Candice in it.' The kid had spent the night, then, at Elijah Tuttle's place as Carson had guessed.

'Come morning you couldn't have followed anyone else's tracks either.'

'Not then, no. I'd seen the wagon and figured I'd come back and wait to see if someone claimed it,' Wesley Short said.

'Which they did,' Carson said. He told Wesley briefly about the night spent in Sterling March's house as they sat watching the two riders ahead of them cross the valley floor.

'Who are they, do you know?' he asked Wesley Short.

'Men who showed up shortly after Mr Prince left on his trip, after Saxon had gotten there, but before the big man with the wagon.'

'The big man's name is Lou Weathers,' Carson told Short.

'I don't care for his looks,' the young cowboy said.

'You'd care for them less up close.'

'Sir,' Wesley Short asked sincerely — it was the first time anyone had used that form of address with Carson for a long time — 'no one's hurt Candice, have they? Or bothered her at all?'

'She wasn't doing any complaining,' was all Carson could tell the young man.

Wesley just nodded a response. He sighed. 'Those two,' he said, lifting his chin toward the riders who were now entering the forest on the far side of the valley, 'are named Curt something and Abel Yardley. They said they were looking for work and would we let them stay until Mr Prince got back so they could ask him. Well, you know how it is, you don't just throw men out, so they stayed in the bunkhouse with us.

'I saw both of them talking to Bill Saxon more than once, like they were all up to something. And they were. I guess their job was to make sure that no one followed after Saxon and Weathers. At least, when I rode out, there they were, following right on my heels.'

'They would have been gone by the time I reached the 9/7,' Carson said.

'You made good time catching up,' Wesley said.

'A Conestoga wagon is not built for speed.'

'No. Well, I'm glad you caught up at all. So now what do we do?'

That was a very difficult question. Carson had no solid answer for young Wesley Short, but their first course of action was obvious.

'Did you ever have the desire to visit a town called Tumble Oaks?'

7

Both Carson and Wesley Short were shivering in their leather jackets before they came within sight of the town. Neither was dressed for this high-mountain weather. The temperature had plummeted; the sky was dark long before sunset as a fresh swarm of black storm clouds moved in, threatening a new blizzard. These hid the tips of the mountain range, shadowed the earth deeply, and crawled slowly across the land, promising trouble.

'At least we don't have to worry about the four of them going any farther any time soon,' Wesley said through chattering teeth. Carson nodded, glancing toward the menacing sky.

'If they can even make Tumble Oaks,' Carson Banner answered. 'The Conestoga they're driving is a clumsy beast, and slow as molasses.'

Wesley Short looked suddenly fearful.

'Maybe we should have stayed closer to the wagon.'

'I think not. It seems that that is what Curt and Abel Yardley had in mind. They have cut some kind of deal with Bill Saxon and Weathers. They're expecting a share of Julian Prince's stolen money. They'll do whatever they can to make sure the wagon makes it through to Tumble Oaks.'

'I guess they'd have to,' Wesley said, unhappily. Maybe he was speculating, as was Carson, that they now probably had four armed men to deal with before they had a hope of rescuing the women and recovering the money. 'How far is it now, do you think?'

Carson lifted his eyes and peered down the rugged slope into the low country. 'I don't know this area any better than you do,' Carson could only answer. 'The first I knew of it, Lige told me it took him two days to get there, but he was traveling with a pack mule and in no hurry to get there.'

'I hope we can find it by nightfall.

I've no wish to spend a night exposed on this mountainside.'

Nor did Carson Banner. They rode on through the gathering gloom, the evening growing steadily colder, until, halted on the rim of a snowy ridge, Wesley lifted a finger and nearly shouted.

'Do you see that? I saw some sort of light ahead.'

Carson nodded. He, too, had seen the flicker of a distant lantern. He did not care at that moment if it was Tumble Oaks or some lonesome farmhouse. Whatever it was, it promised shelter from the cruel night to come.

On horses nearly staggering with exhaustion, they reached the town limits of Tumble Oaks two hours later. It had begun to snow again, and hard. The ragged little town was a welcome sight to the two men, though it could not be described in more generous words than what he had been told — a collection of huts clinging to the side of the mountain like a dying insect.

Muddy roads, now deep in snow, wound

up haphazardly to higher reaches from the main road. Carson had seen mining towns built like that, usually simply because there was limited flat ground to build on. In Tumble Oaks that did not seem to be the problem. The main street was fairly wide with a row of mostly unpainted buildings facing it, all dismal looking, weather-beaten.

It was a sad little place.

It was also extremely welcome just then, at that time of near darkness with another strong storm stretching mighty arms southward and a hard wind blowing.

'First restaurant or first saloon,' Wesley Short said. 'It's all the same to me, so long as we're out of this weather.'

Carson agreed, but he said, 'The second one we come to.' At Wesley Short's quizzical glance, Carson Banner explained himself. 'Anyone else arriving in town tonight is going to automatically want to stop at the first establishment they come across. I don't want to be there to greet them. But,' Carson said, 'let's put these ponies up first; a horse can suffer cold as much a man, and we're surely out of luck without our horses.'

Wesley Short nodded, a little dismally. There was no one out on the street they could ask for directions, and few signs hung from the buildings that weren't so weather-scoured as to be illegible.

They happened upon a man who was leading a pair of horses inside a tall building to get them away from the storm, and they followed along.

The interior of the stable, for that is what it was, was warm with animal heat. The plank walls cut the gusts of cold wind although the old building rattled and whistled before the storm's assault. It was a welcome respite from the weather outside.

'Who are you?' a raspy voice demanded, and they both turned to see a thin man in a bulky buffalo coat emerge from the rear of the stable. It was the man they had seen leading his horses in there. 'And what do you want?'

'A warm place for our ponies to rest up and be fed,' Carson answered. 'Isn't that what you're in business for?'

'Sometimes I don't know what I'm in business for,' the man grumbled. 'People from down on the flatlands come up here and they panic at the first bit of hard weather. Then they all want to rush here. Most times they have it in mind to try to cheat me by slipping their horses out again the first time the sun shines.'

'We're willing to pay in advance,' Carson said, which relieved Wesley Short, who had barely two dollars in his jeans, 'say two days' board and feed?'

'That'll work. Show me the color of your money.'

As they paid the man his advance in his grubby little suitcase-sized office, Wesley Short ventured, 'There'll be some people arriving aboard a Conestoga wagon. Is there any way you could let us know when it comes in?'

'No,' the man said in a definite tone, closing and locking his cash box. 'No way at all, mister. I don't associate myself with nobody else's problems — and you'll soon find out that that's the way it is with every resident of Tumble Oaks. We don't care for outsiders much anyway, and we sure don't want to be mixed up in their situations no matter what they are.'

'The real friendly sort,' Wesley said as he and Carson stood just inside the stable's open double doors, staring out gloomily at the snow which now fell in blankets.

'Can't blame him. When is it ever wise to get mixed up in someone else's affairs — especially a stranger's?'

'You're right, of course.' Wesley still stood, trying to penetrate the falling snow with his eyes. He was waiting for the wagon, for Candice Prince of course. Carson had told him about the wagon's broken wheel hub, and the kid was concerned that it might have snapped again, leaving the travelers marooned on the mountainside.

'Come on,' Carson said, nudging the

kid. 'We're doing no good here. Let's see if we can find a place to hole up ourselves before it gets so bad out here that we get lost trying to cross the street.'

They started forward then through the buffeting wind, the snow swirling around them. It was already ankle deep on the ground, and Carson was right — they did have to find shelter or they'd find themselves no better off than someone stranded in a wagon on the open mountain flanks. Tugging their hats low they trudged into the force of the wind, achieving the plankwalk on the opposite side of the street with some difficulty. There, pressed against the face of a building they were able to catch some relief.

'How can anyone live here?' Wesley Short asked. 'Think of those people up the high road we saw. They can't get out. There's no help if they need it.'

'Mountain people are a little different from you and me,' Carson told him. 'They value their privacy highly, more than any comfort you care to name.'

'Well, we know the kidnappers haven't reached town yet,' a shivering Wesley Short said. 'What do you say we now find a place to get a drink? Somewhere we can ask about food and lodging.'

'It's a plan,' Carson answered. 'Let's ease along the street until we hear some activity. A saloon, even in a place like Tumble Oaks, will be open no matter the weather.'

The storm dampened all sound, closed all vision as it rode roughshod over the poor mountain town, but after walking another block they found a low, unpainted building with light in the windows and the sound of desperate hilarity inside. They managed to open the heavy door of the establishment and slip inside where they immediately became objects of curiosity. Strangers were not a common sight in this isolated community.

Carson led the way directly to a heavy plank bar, glancing around for a sight of Bill Saxon or Lou Weathers, even knowing that the wagon had still not arrived in Tumble Oaks.

'See anyone you know?' Carson asked Wesley Short. He himself had never seen the men named Curt and Abel Yardley except at a great distance. When the kid turned, Carson advised him, 'Don't make it too obvious that you're searching.'

There was no gauging the moods or inclinations of this huddled group of clannish mountain men. A single drunken one of them could set off a lot of trouble for the intruders — which was how they seemed to view Carson and Wesley Short.

The bartender, a porcine man with a split nose, had returned and they ordered a second whiskey. It seemed to be the local custom to drink up as rapidly as possible. Young Wesley Short was not an experienced drinker, and Carson himself had never cultivated the hard liquor habit, so after that drink they decided mutually that they had had enough.

'Any place a man can find a bed and

wait out the storm?' Carson asked the bartender. He was a scowling man; Carson would have wagered that a knife fight had been the cause of his split nose.

'If you're planning on waiting out this storm in bed, you'd better find yourself a widow lady,' the bartender said. 'This one's not going to blow itself out overnight, I'll promise you.'

Carson smiled, not feeling much amused. 'That's all right, then. We need accommodations and food. It's been a long trail for us.'

'We've got one rooming house in this town,' the bartender told them after Carson had taken the time to spread some silver money on the bar in front of him. 'Mrs Todd is the name of the woman running it. It's half a block down on this side of the street. A log building.'

The bartender scraped up the coins Carson had left on the bar and the two turned and walked out the front door without a nod or a glance back. Wesley

Short stood for a moment looking up the street, but there was still no sign of the Conestoga. Carson was beginning to wonder if he had made a mistake, leaving the Prince girls out in this weather. He shook that thought off — they had four men to take care of them. Even if Saxon would be willing to desert Candice, of whom he seemed to have grown weary already, Lou Weathers would not abandon Ruth Price, whom he seemed to believe was his property now.

None of them would be willing to ride away from the money. And who was it that held Julian Prince's stolen cash? That would be important as Carson planned out his next move.

It seemed that the planner, the leader Bill Saxon, must be holding the loot, but Carson had seen and heard hints back at Sterling March's palatial mountain refuge that it might be Ruth Prince who was guarding the money. Candice Prince? No — the little dimwit would have handed the money over to Saxon the moment he asked her for it.

Candice was young and silly, suitable only for a boy her own age, as Saxon had already decided and Wesley Short was convinced.

As for Lou Weathers, he doubted that any one of them would have trusted the big, sloppy, dangerous man with the cash.

That would have to be determined before Carson made his move. Maybe Julian Prince would be grateful if only his daughters were returned to the Nine-Slash-Seven, but that was only a part of the job that Carson Banner had hired on to do. Neither Carson nor John Dancer, his boss, would be satisfied with partial success.

They had been moving as Carson pondered these things — it was no time or place to stand around meditating. Carson now found his back up against a low rough wall which seemed to emanate warmth. There was a very dim light showing through a high window.

'I think this must be the place,' Carson said to Wesley.

'I s-sincerely hope so,' replied Wesley Short, whose teeth were chattering again.

They fumbled for the door latch, found it and eased on through to a low-ceilinged room. Once inside both men immediately removed their jackets. Although it was not particularly warm in the room, the difference between outside and in was terrific.

Looking around they saw no one. There was a small bell on the counter and evidence of a woman's touch around the room. Small statuettes of shepherds and milkmaids stood on shelves, and hand-decorated plates were in wire hangers on the walls.

'I can smell cooking somewhere,' Wesley Short said, nearly salivating. 'Pork, I think.'

It was a welcome smell, Carson Banner agreed. 'But first, let's make sure we know where we are and what we're doing,' Carson advised. 'For all we know, we're interrupting someone's dinner.' Carson rang the little silver bell on the counter.

After the fourth ring they heard

shuffling footsteps and an old woman in carpet slippers, black dress and pink shawl came out to meet them, moving as if her feet hurt her a lot.

Her face sagged at the corners; her arched nose had a pimple at the end of it; one of her eye teeth was black. Her voice was unfriendly, cracked.

'What is it?' she asked in a voice that seemed to expect nothing good to happen, ever.

'Just two traveling men needing a room and some hot food,' Carson replied. Anticipating her next question, he said, 'We have cash money to spend.'

'All right,' she answered as if it were an imposition. 'I have a room for you, and food if you're ready to eat now. Take much time about it and the others will finish it off before you reach the table.'

'We're ready now,' Carson told her. 'When would you like to be paid?'

'Before you get to eating,' the woman snapped.

The money Carson handed her did

little to soften her manner, but she indicated the way with a nod of her head and shuffled off along a narrow corridor toward a room where the smell of good cooking intensified. There were six men around a low table, mostly bearded, rough-looking with the elbows of their shirts out and their hands meaty and raw.

Carson seated himself at the table and reached for the platter of fried pork chops that had been served. There was also mashed potatoes and dark gravy and some biscuits which had been burnt on the bottom but were still tasty with butter. The men around the table had given Carson no more than the casual glance he expected and returned their attention to their knives and forks.

Seated across the table from Wesley Short was one man who seemed to take more than a casual interest in the kid. He had his hat tugged low as he ate, and a narrow, almost wolfish face. There were blue half-moons under his eyes. His lips were full, his face whiskered. He looked at Wesley, looked again, but said nothing. The man's glance also strayed to take in Carson Banner, but he seemed to show no interest in him.

It was not until the meal was finished and Carson and Wesley Short had made their way along the narrow, dark corridor to their room that Wesley spoke up.

'That was Curt,' Wesley said.

'Who?'

'That man across the table from us. That was Curt, the one who was riding with Abel Yardley. The ones following the wagon.'

'Are you sure?' Carson asked as they settled on to their facing bunks after lighting the lamp.

'Yes, I'm sure,' Wesley said emphatically. 'You saw his face; do you think that's the kind of man I'd forget? What does it mean, Carson? How did he get here ahead of us?'

'Maybe they're all here,' Carson said, tugging off his boots.

'But how . . . ?'

'Remember, the last time the wagon broke down they cut the horses loose and rode off toward Sterling March's. Perhaps the wagon didn't make it as far as Jingo thought it would and they had to cut the horses out again and ride for Tumble Oaks.'

'That means that Candice . . . all of them are right here in this hotel,' Wesley said with a kind of boyish excitement.

'There's a chance that's so,' Carson agreed.

'We've got to find them,' Wesley believed.

'To what purpose?' Carson asked from behind a yawn. 'We can't rescue anybody, reclaim Julian Prince's money here with four armed men to protect it.'

Frustrated, Wesley Short blurted out, 'You must have some kind of plan, Carson! This is supposed to be your line of work, after all. Just what do you intend to do about matters?'

Carson Banner did not respond. He figured he had done everything, all the thinking he could do for that day. The room was cold, the bed warm. He had drifted off to an exhausted sleep before Wesley Short had even finished his rant.

8

Carson didn't have to crawl out of bed and look outside the following morning to know that the storm had settled in, that it had snowed the night long. There was that heavy feel in the air and a slight sluggishness in his blood that indicated it was not the time to work, to travel. It must have been this way that primitive men reacted to such weather. It was time to let winter have its way, to curl up with your wife or your dogs and go back to sleep.

Carson could not do that, however; his work would not wait until the snow melted.

Wesley Short had been correct the night before when he pointed out that he, they, still seemed to have no plan for what must be done. Carson doubted there was an effective plan he could come up with. Still, a man has to try. They would

125

not have many other chances. If the storm cleared again the men they were pursuing would be gone with their stolen money — especially since now they had probably heard from Curt that he had seen Wesley Short, the Nine-Slash-Seven rider and another man in the inn. Curt had not recognized Carson, but from his description it was likely that Bill Saxon and Lou Walters would. They knew Carson had been riding toward Tumble Oaks.

They would know, at least, that two men were on their trail and that this could not augur well for them. Trying to predict the outlaws' move was not simple, but Carson was guessing that by now the four had held a consultation, and two of them at least — Curt and Abel Yardley — would be in favor of letting the women fend for themselves while they made their escape.

Bill Saxon, judging from what Carson had seen of the blond man, would be likely to agree with them — he found the young Candice Prince to be more trouble than she was worth. The game was over; the charade that they were all striking out toward Oregon was no longer even plausible, not with the Conestoga broken down again, not with the heavy snow in the mountain passes.

Their thoughts had to be on waiting to make a break for warmer parts at the first opportunity. If necessary they would take care of anyone following them out in open country where that crime would never be witnessed.

And Carson would be alone in his pursuit — he had no idea that young Wesley Short would ride away from the rescue of Candice, having found her again.

What was there to hold the four robbers from having their way, and leaving at first opportunity? Only one thing that Carson could imagine.

They did not have the money in hand.

Carson still held the notion that somehow Ruth Prince had taken charge of the money or hidden it. That would slow the men down, but it would not bode well for Ruth. There was no doubt they would try in a very rough way to make her give up the money.

Carson Banner was frowning as he stamped into his boots, put on his leather jacket and went out, leaving the exhausted Wesley Short asleep in their room.

The corridor was chilly, but not cold. There was a fire burning somewhere in the rooming house. Someone making breakfast? He was disabused of that notion after asking an older, gnarled man who looked like a long-time habitué of the place.

'Mrs Todd don't provide breakfast for her guests,' the old man said, slipping up his red suspenders over the shoulders of his heavy blue wool shirt. 'She don't like rising early. You'll have to get along with what the rest of us do.'

'What's that?' Carson asked.

'There's always coffee on at the saloon,' the old man advised him, 'and it's never closed.'

Carson nodded. 'How's the weather outside?'

He got a smile in response to his question. 'You were here last night; you know how it is this morning. You'll be all right getting to the saloon, stranger. Just stay under the awnings — if they haven't broken down — and follow the tracks in the snow.'

Carson thanked the man and passed through the office space to the front door. The heavy door opened easily. He guessed that the wind had abated overnight and was no longer pressing against it. Outside snow commanded the skies and the streets of the town. There were drifts up over the plank-walks and crowding the buildings. The street could not be seen nor used for traffic; it was unmarked by passage.

True to the old man's word, however, there was a line of tramped snow leading down the street toward the saloon he and Wesley Short had visited the night before. He was wary of entering the place. Three of the men in

Saxon's gang he knew. The one he had not seen was Abel Yardley, who he knew only from Wesley's description: a tall, thin man with a red face.

Did it matter? Perhaps. Abel Yardley could be one of those men who shot first regardless of the consequences. There were more than a few of these roaming around in the West. In a town where both men were strangers, it was possible that the locals would simply ignore such a shooting, figuring it was none of their business.

Carson waded on through the snow, which was perpetually falling, not in sheets but in curtains, Tumble Oaks becoming even more smothered by the storm. Carson was now willing to believe that Sterling March's house, which was even higher up the mountainside, had seen nine-foot drifts the year before.

As Wesley Short had asked — why did these people choose to live here? Carson thought he knew. A man who has wandered far enough eventually finds himself at a point in life when he is tired of wandering, refuses to go farther, and when he is stopped in such a place, there he will remain. Time can extinguish the wandering urge.

Carson had to duck a bit to enter the saloon wearing his hat. Heads turned his way, most of them to make sure the door was closed again quickly. The faces watching Carson were curious, but not interested enough to watch him long as he walked across the room to the rough counter of the bar.

A good portion of the men were drinking coffee from heavy wooden mugs; about half of them were already at their whiskey. Why not? They had nothing else to do, nowhere to go. There was no talk of the weather. It was here and it was a dominant force of life. No amount of talking about it would change a thing.

Besides, the residents of Tumble Oaks were used to it, had lived through many years of it, and it was nothing remarkable enough to comment on.

Carson beckoned the barman and got his own cup of hot, bitter coffee. Most of the men were gathered in silent groups around the tables, a few were strung along the bar, talking. Carson saw only one man who seemed more out of place than he himself felt.

At the far end of the bar, nearly facing him was a tall, thin man with an extremely red face. He was younger than the average resident of Tumble Oaks, seemed more nervous and upset than the resigned local men. He was further set apart by his Texas-style garb, that of a sometimes cattleman and not of a mountain denizen.

He had dark eyes fixed on Carson Banner along the length of the bar. Carson decided that he had now seen the last of the gang, Abel Yardley. Of Bill Saxon and Lou Weathers nothing had been seen, nor had the women been visible in Tumble Oaks. Could those four be staying somewhere other than the inn, or had something else happened to them along the trail

— something that he and Wesley Short had not guessed?

That was a chilling thought. The wagon could have tumbled down the mountainside. The four bandits could have had a falling-out which left only Curt and Yardley alive. And the women — had they simply been abandoned? Maybe the two men — or all four of them — had agreed that they had no more use for Candice and Ruth Prince.

Carson signaled for another cup of the strong coffee and chased his conjectures away. He would have liked to talk to Abel Yardley, to learn what he knew, but Yardley obviously now had other thoughts in mind.

Yardley now stood at the end of the bar, opening the gate of his Colt revolver's cylinder and checking the loads in an obvious manner. It was clear to Carson who the display was intended for.

Yardley turned from the bar and started toward the door. With his eyes he issued an invitation — or a challenge. Carson let the man go

133

outside to stand in the snow as he slowly finished his coffee. There was no sense to Yardley's challenge, except that he, like Carson, must have known that the situation must come to shooting sooner or later.

Yardley wished to make it sooner.

The eyes of several more alert men followed Carson as he made his own way to the door. Yardley had been too blatant in his behavior not to have brought some attention to himself. No one stirred, spoke out loud, or whispered. This was Tumble Oaks, and what outsiders did was their own business and none of the town's.

Stepping outside, Carson scanned the street for Abel Yardley, but if he was around, he could not be seen through the whirl and wash of the heavy snow. Probably, Carson thought, after standing out there for long minutes Yardley had given it up and returned to the inn. But that was not the case. Yardley appeared like a winter specter from out of the swirl of cold, heavy cotton. He yelled something, yelled again, but Carson could not hear him above the wash of the storm, and he waited until Yardley had taken a few more strides toward him and could be understood.

'What do you want with me?' Yardley bellowed.

'I didn't say I wanted anything from you,' Carson hollered back, feeling that it was a stupid way to hold a conversation. But then, Yardley wasn't really interested in conversation. He was working himself up into a state of mind where he would have the nerve to draw on Carson.

'You been to Texas?' Yardley called.

'Yes.'

'And you don't know me from down there?'

'No, I don't!' Carson shouted.

'Then you're not a lawman?' The wind had risen again and it twisted and muted Abel Yardley's words.

'No, I'm not,' Carson said, watching Yardley's right hand all the time. The man hadn't waited out here just to converse.

'That makes it better,' Yardley said at the top of his lungs. Other than the two of them there was not a single person to be seen along the length of the storm-lashed street. 'Then no one at all is going to care much what happens to you!'

Yardley had now worked himself up to a fever pitch, and as Carson Banner had seen before, the overexcitement had rattled his own nerves. Yardley's hand was not smooth as it went toward his holster. Maybe, too, the cold had numbed him slightly, but his draw was clumsy and his shot inaccurate. Carson held his ground, drawing smoothly. His pistol bucked in his hand and he saw Yardley tagged and swung around by the heavy impact of the .44 slug.

Yardley staggered a little and then dropped into the four-foot-deep snow. Carson waited, cocking his pistol once more, and it was a good thing that he had. For suddenly Abel Yardley rose from the snowdrift, hatless, eyes wide, blood staining his chest. Carson didn't wait for Yardley to trigger off again. He shot the snow phantom where he stood and Yardley again descended into the snow. This time he sagged away slowly. Carson knew the man would not rise again.

He waded through the heavy snow, breaking a path to where Yardley lay. He could see the man, curled, gun hand empty, life leaking out of him, staining the snow, his eyes still open to the cold and bluster of the storm.

'You should have stayed in Texas,' Carson Banner said, holstering his gun before he made his heavy way back to the plankwalk.

Still there was not a single person outside the buildings looking toward the excitement. But then, thinking back, Carson himself had barely been able to hear the gunshots above the wind noise and the muffling of the snowfall, and the residents of Tumble Oaks were indifferent to the troubles of outsiders.

★ ★ ★

Back in his room in the boarding house Carson found Wesley Short, barely risen. The kid sat on the edge of the bunk, his boots held loosely in his hand as if he had barely the energy to tug them on and start a new day. Still his eyes lit eagerly as Carson re-entered the room.

'Any luck this morning?'

'If you're asking if I found the women, no. No luck.'

Wesley Short's face sagged with disappointment. Perhaps he, like Carson, was starting to have doubts that Candice and Ruth had made it to Tumble Oaks at all.

'If it comes to a fight,' Carson said, 'when it comes to a fight, I should say, the odds grew in our favor just a little.' Carson sat down on his own bunk.

'Oh? How's that?' Wesley asked with slightly revived interest.

Carson told him simply, without embellishment, that he had been forced to shoot down Abel Yardley in the street.

'What did he tell you before he died?' Wesley asked, now bending forward at the waist eagerly. Carson had to deflate the young man's hopes once again.

'Not a word. He didn't give me any clue at all as to where the others were.' Of course they knew where Curt was — somewhere in this very inn. Carson wondered how close the two bad men had been. They were saddle partners. That probably did not matter at all. Carson had the idea that they would have to shoot it out with Curt the next time they encountered him, no matter what.

'Well,' Wesley Short said at length. 'There's only one thing we can do right now, isn't there? We have to go out there and try to find the women, don't we, Carson?'

'I suppose we do,' Carson Banner said, standing. It was a lovely day for it. If they did find the women somehow, Carson knew they would also find some armed men with them, guarding not only the women and the stolen money but their own freedom and lives as well. It would take a small war to pry them out of wherever they were holed up.

They had passed the point when any surrender was possible. The first shots of battle had been fired.

9

Carson found himself envying the primitive man asleep in his cave or his teepee, the hogan with his dogs or his wife. It was a brutal day, getting no better as they tried to search the unknown town for two men with a violent streak in them and the will to use their guns against anyone who attempted to thwart them.

Saxon and his men now could have only one obvious plan. To obtain saddle horses from somewhere and strike out for the low country with the stolen money in their saddle-bags. Assuming the weather permitted such an adventure, which it did not look like it was about to do. Which made now the time to capture them. Warm weather would send the thieves scurrying away from the mountains.

The women, Carson believed, no

longer fit into the thieves' plans. It was obvious to Carson from watching Saxon at March's estate that he had no interest in Candice any longer and could not even feign concern about the young girl's feelings. Lou Weathers was a different story. He had offered his protection to Ruth on more than one occasion within Carson's hearing. Ruth seemed to disdain the big, brutal man, but perhaps she was playing a waiting game, willing to utilize the violent, bumbling oaf as long as she could as a defender.

There was no telling. She was a woman, and they were clever at their machinations. If Ruth was, somehow, in possession of the money, she might want Lou Weathers around to protect her interest. An occasional smile would be enough to buy his loyalty.

'How are we going to do this?' Wesley Short asked, as they stood outside in the whip and drive of the snow-clotted wind.

'Any idea you might have is as good

as any I have,' Carson shouted back. 'I don't think we can do much but check every building up one side of the street and down the other.'

He had been told that the town had only the one poor inn for travelers. He was also certain that none of them could have an acquaintance in Tumble Oaks. None of the four had ever been in the town before. What about Abel Yardley or Curt? Had one of them an old friend from Texas here — perhaps a wanted man who had chosen to hide out in this remote mountain village?

It was too much of a guessing game to play — all they could do was begin their search, knowing it was also possible that none of the people from the wagon had even made it this far, that only Curt and Yardley had survived to travel on to Tumble Oaks. More guesses. Carson put all of them out of his mind and the two moved on, knocking on the doors of closed and locked businesses, entering the premises of unfriendly shopkeepers along the cold street. They were not endearing themselves to the citizens of Tumble Oaks.

Now and then the snow clouds would part enough so that Carson had a view of the uplands where scattered old shanties rested along the snaky, snow-deep trails. Wesley had wondered what sort of people would live up there, precariously clinging to the side of the long canyons. Carson found himself wondering the same things as their fruitless search continued. Perhaps, he thought, they were looking in all of the wrong places.

A mountain man they encountered in a hardware store was angry enough to chase them out of his business with a rifle. They had not even been able to convince him that they were honest shoppers.

Tough town for strangers — Tumble Oaks.

They again found the stable where they had left their horses, and the sour proprietor watched as they checked them. He seemed to know they were up to something else as if the town had some sort of mysterious underground method of communications. Maybe it was simply their manner.

Wesley Short, especially, was looking for something, obviously. The team from the wagon, for one thing. Those horses had to have been put up somewhere. If not here, where? He went so far as to ask the stable hand a question before Carson could muzzle him.

'Is there another stable in this town?'

'Not so's you'd notice,' the suspicious man snarled. 'Why? Don't you like the way I'm treating your horses? If that's the case, you're welcome to take them out again.'

Carson took the time to soothe the ruffled feathers of the stableman, explaining that the kid was just curious. Barely mollified, the man got back to raking out the stalls, keeping his eyes on Carson and Wesley as they ran through the ritual of currying their horses. The man seemed to think they were using up his heat and was hardly sorry to see them go out into the cold, stormy day once again. Wesley Short was quick with his apology.

'I just thought that it was worth asking.'

'I suppose it was,' Carson replied, letting it go at that.

They walked another half a block through weather so miserable it was difficult to keep from trembling with the cold, to even see through the storm clouds which seemed to be not only above and around them, but at their feet with their intense flurries.

They had decided to brave its full force once more to cross the street toward the far side, continuing their search, when the man known as Curt met them nearly face to face. The bandit was crossing the street in the opposite direction, presumably to check on his own pony, stabled in the same barn as their animals.

'Hold up there,' Wesley Short said,

grabbing Curt's coat sleeve. 'I want to talk to you!'

Curt didn't want to talk to him. He batted Wesley's hand away and stepped aside, bringing his pistol up.

The gun flashed hot red and yellow, reflecting off the white snow around them, and Carson saw Wesley Short turn, his hand going to his side just above the hip bone.

'Don't shoot him, Carson!' Wesley hollered out, but his words were as ineffective against Carson Banner's instincts as they had been with Curt. 'We need . . . '

Curt had shifted the muzzle of his revolver in Carson's direction after shooting Wesley, but the bandit could not aim at two targets at once, and Carson had already slipped his Colt from it's nestling holster and fired twice, jerking Curt where he stood into a sort of epileptic dance. Then as an ashen-faced Wesley Short watched, the bad man slid away into the snowdrifts and breathed his last in the center of that wind-blown, frozen street.

'We needed the man . . . ' Wesley Short was panting. He was bent over at the waist, his hand, where he clenched his wound, leaking blood from between the fingers.

'In a perfect world,' Carson said as he looped his arm around the injured cowboy, 'but this is not such. I wasn't going to let him kill me hoping he'd talk to us. Why would he?'

'I suppose it's just . . . ' Wesley was panting as Carson got the kid the rest of the way across the street and up on to the plankwalk on that side. 'Candice . . . you know, Carson?'

'I know,' Carson said, assisting Wesley back along the street toward their room at the boarding house. He also knew that there was no way on earth Curt could have been convinced to tell them where the others were — if he even knew their location, which Carson was beginning to doubt he had.

It looked now as if Curt and Abel Yardley had been the ones cut out of the deal once Tumble Oaks had been reached. Or before that. But that was another guess, and Carson was plain tired of these guessing games.

For his next job, he vowed he would request a simple task — one bad man, one certain hiding place, no complications. But he knew John Dancer, his boss, would tell him that Carson was losing the spirit of fun in the game.

Dancer would be right. None of this was fun for Carson Banner as he walked the shivering, injured man to the inn, ushered him down the hall to their room and practically dropped Wesley on to his bunk. Carson had nothing at all against the kid, but he was beginning to regret that their paths had crossed. Wesley Short was making matters no easier for him.

'All right,' Carson growled, 'tug your shirt off. Let's see what the damage is.'

Wesley needed some assistance getting his shirt unbuttoned and pulled off. There was a fearful expression in his eyes as he haltingly asked Carson, 'How does it . . . look?'

'I've seen worse,' Carson answered. He'd never found that the answer satisfied an injured man, but he could think of nothing else.

'Looks like the bullet didn't tag anything but meat above your hip and then passed on through. Hell,' he said with a grin, 'that was probably mostly fat anyway.'

Wesley's lip barely twitched in the semblance of a smile. It's hard to see the humor in things when you're in pain and bleeding.

'Let's get that blood cleaned away so that I can see better. Probably I'll just plug the hole and bind you up at the waist. You should be all right.'

'Do what you think is best,' Wesley said tensely. 'I don't have another choice, do I?'

'No. You don't.'

'I still think we should have tried to talk to the man,' Wesley Short persisted as Carson cleaned his wound with soap, water and a room towel.

'I don't think he would have stopped

shooting just to talk — and neither do you.'

'I guess not. What I meant is . . . this is getting awfully frustrating, Carson. I mean, even a day ago we knew where the girls were even if we had no plan for rescuing them.'

'We have two fewer guns to worry about now,' Carson reminded the kid. 'Maybe our luck has turned.'

'Do you believe that?' Wesley asked. Carson nodded.

'I have to.'

'I suppose we at least know that they can't leave the area now — not in this weather. No one could.'

Carson nodded again. He still kept the possibility in mind that the two women might not have made it as far as Tumble Oaks at all. Oddly, he placed his faith in big Lou Weathers having kept them alive and safe. The man was smitten with Ruth Prince; that was obvious. Maybe he saw himself with half of the stolen money in his pockets running off to San Francisco or Denver with his happy young bride. The big dope had never seen the way Ruth looked at him.

With the wound clean, Carson could see that he had been right. The outlaw's bullet had bored a neat hole through Wesley Short's side just above the hip bone, and at that range it had bruised the flesh badly, torn it some, but there were no major blood vessels in the area and as bad as the bleeding must seem to Wesley, it was not that severe. As Carson had told the kid, he had seen worse.

'Sorry, Carson,' Wesley said as Carson Banner wound a torn sheet from his bed tightly around the blond kid's waist. 'I'll slow you down now.'

'No, you won't. Because if I go out again, you're not going.'

'I have to . . . '

'No, you don't. You have to stay here and rest up. As you just said, you'll slow me down. I value having another gun on my side, but not enough to carry you along, wondering if you're going to faint or be left behind if I have to run.'

'So I just lie here?'

'That's what you do. Besides, I have no idea where I'm going and if anything can be accomplished. I'll try to have Mrs Todd send some broth over to you. I don't think she's the nosy type — no one in Tumble Oaks seems to be, but I'll tell her you slipped on a patch of ice. Keep your body covered up with a blanket. I'll clean the rest of the blood up before I go.'

'What are you going to do, Carson?'

'I don't really have an idea, but anything is better than sitting here spoon-feeding you.'

'So you're going back out into the weather to look for the women.' Wesley Short shook his head in wonder. 'You're a brave man, Carson Banner.'

'Not so's you'd notice it,' Carson answered. 'You're forgetting one thing, Wesley. I'm getting paid to do this.'

But not enough, Carson decided as he stepped out once again into the frigid day. He had one stop to make before he got back to work. He had traveled long enough dressed improperly for the conditions. He meant to buy himself a heavy winter coat. A strong wind was gusting out of the north as he made his way toward the general store, but the snow, thankfully, was holding back. Carson could see nearly the length of the street in the clear air.

Two or three men from the saloon had emerged to look at the clearing skies with a kind of superstitious wonder. None of them, least of all Carson Banner, believed the storm's hesitation would last long. Carson purchased a heavy woolen coat from the man in the general store whose look said that he thought Carson was a fool for riding the high country in only his leather jacket in the first place.

Now more warmly clad, he walked the length of the street and peered in the various shops they had detoured around earlier when Wesley had gotten shot. Carson had the luck he had expected. No luck.

Out of solid ideas, he crossed the street again, following the deep groove he and Wesley Short had made in their earlier passing. The same sour man was inside the stable, not working but making use of his shovel as a resting post.

'What is it now?' the stable hand asked as if Carson were a constant annoying presence in his life.

'Do you recall us asking about a Conestoga wagon?' Carson asked. 'Well, I'm going to tell you something honestly.' The stableman's eyes showed no interest. Carson plunged ahead. 'A group of men robbed my friend and myself on the trail. They took our wagon and team from us, and that's who we've been looking for. I lost a good team of four bay horses along with a lot of goods. I need to find them and I'm willing to pay a reward for those horses.'

'Do you see your horses here?' the man asked. 'No, well neither do I. I got nothing to tell you, Mr. I'm sorry for your misery, but it's none of my own.'

The response was typical of Tumble Oaks. Well, Carson thought, it was worth trying. The word 'reward' generally perked up a man's ears. But it seemed the man genuinely knew nothing.

Where did that leave him? Nowhere. He was stuck nowhere, going nowhere. Yet if the four — Saxon, Weathers and the women — had come into town at all someone must have noticed them. He looked up at the sound of happy shouts. A group of kids, bundled to their ears, were playing on the disused main street, using a sheet of wood as a sled.

Now, these were a different sort of witness than the average Tumble Oaks citizen. What's more, kids, as Carson knew, see everything. They might not process it as adults do, but they are always alert to strange, new sights. And they were just as susceptible to bribery as their elders.

He approached the kids, who had started a snowball fight, making maximum use of the storm's brief respite.

Coming up to the kids — there were five or six of them gathered around — he was met by stony glares. Whenever a grown-up approached them it was sure to mean the end to fun in their eyes. Carson put on his best fatherly smile. That had no positive effect. The oldest boy there was about ten years old, at a guess, the youngest no more than five or six. There were no girls with them.

'Hello, men,' Carson said, tipping his hat back. 'I've got a small problem you might be able to help me out with.' He unfolded his hand to reveal a scattering of silver coins. Their eyes brightened. They were each calculating how many sweets they could buy with so much money.

'Wha' d'ya want?' the ten-year-old asked warily. He was already a well-indoctrinated citizen of Tumble Oaks. Trust no outsider.

'Oh, it's nothing much,' Carson said letting the coins slip and rub together in his gloved hand. He took them all in with a glance. 'You see, men, I was supposed to meet my friends here, but we got separated in the storm. Two men and two women, they were. They had four horses with them.'

'Ain't seen nothin',' the oldest boy said. He had been well trained in the mountain ways, it seemed.

'I seen 'em, I seen 'em!' the youngest boy said, waving his hand eagerly. 'On'y last night I seen 'em! They went right by my house.'

'Did they now?' Carson asked, turning all of his attention to the six-year-old, who was wearing a patched jacket, a red muffler tied up to his chin and a leather cap. 'And where is your house?'

'Don't tell 'im nuffin', Ralphie. He's probably a sheriff or somethin'.'

'I promise I'm not,' Carson told them. 'I just want to find my friends. Where's your house, Ralphie?'

'Right there,' the six-year-old said, pointing a finger in a knitted mitten upslope toward where the winding trails led deeper into the snow-covered hills.

'See that green house? They went right by us.'

'Two men?' Carson asked, wanting to be sure.

'And two lovely ladies wearing fancy clothes like you see in the mail-order books. An' they had four bay horses like they was a team.'

'That sounds like them,' Carson said, rising. 'They must have had some trouble back along the trail.'

'Ah, it's all mush,' the oldest boy said disparagingly. 'Ain't nobody lives past Ralphie's house up there except for Old Man Sanders, and he don't never have company. Ma says it's because he's grumpy.'

'Well, it's a place to start looking,' Carson said. 'Ralphie, boys, I thank you all for trying to help a man in need of help.' Carson passed out nickels and dimes all around to the eager, waiting hands. Who knew, that might even teach the kids a little about helping strangers — even in Tumble Oaks.

Shrieking, the kids ran off toward the

nearest store to spend their new-found riches, leaving Carson standing alone in the middle of the street, looking up toward the craggy, snow-draped heights beyond the town.

Somewhere up there were the two women he had come to find and the stolen money. As well as two brutal men with guns.

10

Carson returned to the stable to fetch his gray horse. The man in the stable was no more pleased to see him than he had been on any of Carson's previous visits. Carson thought of asking the hand if he knew a man named Sanders, but he knew what sort of a response he would get.

'You leaving?' the stableman asked.

'Just going out for a ride.'

'Nice day for it,' the man said sarcastically.

'My horse needs exercise every day or he gets stale,' Carson said, tightening his cinches.

'When it starts snowing again, you'll find that he gets stale real quick.'

There was nothing to be said to that. Carson led the gray out of its stall, mounting in the open doorway of the stable. Then he looked down the length of the snow-deep street, sighing. There was going to be brutal work for the horse that day. Carson rode past the two humps in the snow, thinking that there would be some surprise and a little work for the citizens of Tumble Oaks when the snow melted.

Riding out of the east end of town the going got no easier. The skies had grown leaden again, the wind was brisk and very cold. The winding road leading into the highlands was deep in snow, and likely there were patches of ice underfoot. Well, Carson was riding a good horse, and this was the reason he had bought the sturdy animal — you just never knew in his business. He didn't need a racehorse to track down outlaws, but steady willingness.

Using Ralphie's green house as a landmark, Carson guided the horse higher up the twisting trail. Once, as he was rounding a sheltered, rocky bend in the road, he came upon a patch of ground, almost clear of snow in this protected spot. There they were — the tracks of four horses moving together.

Carson was not that much of a tracker, but he was certain the hoof prints could not have been more than a day old. He rode on into the gusting wind.

On the porch of the green house a fat woman in a shawl stood, looking down toward Tumble Oaks. Ralphie's mother, wanting to yell for the boy to come home, knowing her voice would not reach that far?

She would be concerned about the boy, knowing that the storm could set in again at any time. Carson doubted Ralphie's homecoming would be a gentle one. Probably his mother had let the boy go out to play while the weather briefly held clear, but Ralphie, feeling alone, had made his way down the long trail to find others to play with.

Carson thought of stopping, of telling her that Ralphie was fine, and of asking where Old Man Sanders' place could be found. Neither idea seemed to be a good one on second thought.

It was another half-mile up the twisting, narrowing trail before Carson sighted a gray, sagging shack set in a cleft between two low ridges. If the man known as Sanders had been looking for seclusion, he had managed to find it. Few people knew that Tumble Oaks existed; no one not from the immediate area would suspect this poor little house rested hidden away up here.

Who could Sanders be? Carson was still stuck with the notion of an outlaw on the run, hiding from the law, though he had no evidence to support that idea. 'Old Man Sanders', the boys called him, but what did old mean to a ten-year-old boy? Eighty or thirty? Either would be old to a kid. In other places Carson had been, kids often hung the title 'old man' or 'old lady' on someone they were wary of or had seldom seen. Someone about whom something was different. That could very well be the case here. Carson only knew that he now had three gunmen to concern himself with. He approached the house more than a little wary.

There was no one in the yard on this

cold morning, but in a tilted lean-to behind the house Carson spotted the bay horses — all four of them. So they were all there unless someone had made the unlikely choice to walk down the hill to Tumble Oaks, or they had traded the horses to Sanders for some of his own. Neither seemed likely, and again Carson found that he was only guessing, grabbing for any possibility only because he did not totally understand the situation and never had. Julian Prince had given Carson a simple explanation of the plan his daughters and the bad men had hatched, but Julian Prince could only speak of what he knew or had guessed himself.

That did not matter right now — none of it did. Carson sat shivering in the wind. A few scattered snowflakes had begun to fall. What was he to do? It seemed mad to simply rush the house or walk up to it without a plan, yet when again would he have the chance? When would he be so near to them again, if ever?

It was then that the front door to the

shanty opened and a woman in a red cloak and hood stepped out on to the sagging porch.

Ruth Prince.

She stood surveying the yard for a time, looking up toward the sky and at the rocky crags surrounding the Sanders place, then almost delicately, she stepped off the porch and began walking aimlessly around the yard.

Was this the opportunity Carson had been waiting for? Maybe not, but it was an opportunity. He began walking his gray horse toward the house. When Ruth had gotten far enough from the house, Carson turned his horse toward her. The gray's footfalls were soft against the snow, and Ruth, who was picking her way across the yard on unsteady feet, holding her skirt high, did not see or hear him until Carson was nearly on top of her.

'You!' Ruth gasped in a near-whisper.

'It's me, Ruth,' Carson said, edging his horse up beside her, blocking a path of escape.

However, Ruth did not move. Her eyes flickered toward the house where a faint curlicue of smoke from the chimney rose higher, merging with the gray of the low clouds.

'If they see you . . . ' Ruth Prince gasped.

'You're right. It wouldn't be pretty to watch. But for right now, you're the only one who can see me, and I'd like to know what's going on.'

'What do you mean?' Ruth asked, still almost breathlessly. 'You obviously know all about matters.'

'Do I?' Carson smothered a laugh. He knew almost nothing, he had decided. He got right to it. 'Are all the men in the house, Ruth?'

'No.' She shook her head. Her dark eyes met Carson's, asking questions he did not understand. 'Only Sanders. He used to be friends with Abel Yardley. He wanted to know where Yardley had gotten to. Saxon and Lou volunteered to ride down and have a look around. Sanders said he would go himself, but he didn't much like showing his face, even in a town like Tumble Oaks. I think there's a murder warrant out for him.'

'I didn't see Saxon or Lou on the way up, nor any sign that they'd passed.'

'You came up from the east, then. There's another trail down the other way,' Ruth said. 'I've been keeping my eyes and ears open to these details in case we got the chance to make our escape.'

'You and Candice? Is she willing to go now?' Carson asked.

'She is.' Ruth gestured toward the house. 'Look where all of this has landed us. Even Candice can see that we're going nowhere with these men. Her love for Bill Saxon has lost all of its luster.'

Carson brightened a little. 'Then I can get you out of here. I didn't want to be fighting with a struggling woman all the way down the hillside.' He paused, then added, 'You might tell her that Wesley Short is waiting for her in town.'

'Wes?' Ruth said with astonishment.

'That's right. He cared enough about Candice to follow you all the way out here and get himself shot for her sake.' At the startled look in Ruth's eyes, Carson added, 'It's not a critical wound — I left him resting in the boarding house down there. If what you're telling me is true, we should be able to make our escape using the east trail again. I can't see a reason for Saxon and Weathers, being strangers, to risk trying a new trail when they are familiar with the one they just traveled.'

'I suppose you're right,' Ruth said hesitantly. 'We have to try it soon, don't we? Before they get back from town.'

'Yes, we do.'

'There's one other problem,' Ruth said.

'Sanders?' Carson said. 'Yes, I was thinking of that little hitch in the plan. What was he doing when you left? Not sitting holding a shotgun?'

'No. Just pottering around in the kitchen. Why would he think he needed a gun?'

'I don't know. But he's a man on the run and they tend to remain cautious at all times. Can you bring Candice out of the house, too?'

'I don't think Sanders would let both of us out at once. He knows I won't run away and leave my sister, so he didn't mind me stepping out for a minute.'

That left Carson without a choice. He would have to brace the man, who was very probably a killer on the run. Well, if he was careful, Carson thought, he would at least have the advantage of surprise. Even the door opening should not alert him if he expected Lou Weathers and Bill Saxon to return soon. After that, well . . . it was certain Sanders would have a weapon close to hand inside the house. A hunted man takes as few chances as possible.

'If it has to be done, it has to be done,' Carson said out loud, and Ruth knew what he meant. 'There's one more thing I have to know, Ruth,' he told her seriously. She looked up at him worried. 'Have you got the stolen money?'

170

She was aghast. 'Me! Why would I have it? How could I possibly have gotten it?' She held the fingertips of both hands to her breast. It was impossible to disbelieve her shock and dismay.

'Sorry. It was just a thought I had. A possibility.'

'You think I would steal money from my own father?'

'It was just a thought,' Carson said again. Ruth would not be soothed.

'Is that why you're in this at all, why you've chased us over hill and dale? For the money?'

Carson tired of the accusation in the woman's eyes. Sharply, he told her, 'Your father hired me to recover his money and bring his daughters home. I might be able to finish half of the job today, with your help, but I need to consider the other part of it.'

'All right, then,' Ruth said with an apologetic sigh. 'I suppose I can understand that.' She hesitated. 'What do we do now?'

'The only thing there is to do — we

pay a visit to Old Man Sanders.'

'What's my part in it?'

Briefly Carson told her what he had decided. Ruth nodded her understanding unhappily, and agreed to do as he asked. She started back toward the house and Carson stepped down from the gray horse. He needed only his own two feet for this plan to succeed — or to fail. Waiting a second or two before he started after Ruth, he checked the action of his Colt. It was rare, but weapons had been known to freeze up in this kind of weather. It would not do to have that happen just now.

He followed in Ruth's footprints, saw her enter the house, leaving the door open an inch or two. He was near enough to hear Ruth when she spoke as instructed.

'I think I saw them coming along the trail. They'll be here in a few minutes.'

'Did they bring Abel with them?' a strange, hoarse voice inquired.

'I couldn't tell. They were pretty far off when I first saw them,' Ruth replied.

The man responded with some sort of broken tale about him and Abel Yardley down in Texas. Carson was paying no attention to the story as he slipped silently on to the broken porch. His heart rate had increased; blood sang in his ears. He was gripping his Colt revolver too tightly. Dammit, he was scared!

But there was no help for that, not just then. He waited until he heard Ruth doing as she had been told to do: getting her sister out of the path of any bullets.

'Darn it,' Carson heard Ruth say, 'I've lost a button off my sleeve. Help me look for it, Candice. It's right over here somewhere.'

It was time. Carson didn't like it but it was time. Someone had said that an idea that is not followed through on is no better than a dream. It was not Carson Banner's time to dream.

He marched up to the front door, not concerned with stealth. Hearing approaching boots, Sanders would have to believe that it was his own men returning — Ruth had announced their arrival.

That misapprehension lasted only a fraction of a second, enough to slow Sanders' hand reaching for the rifle on the table. Carson was ready, pistol cocked, half-aimed when he stepped inside the cabin. As Sanders' hand clutched the receiver of the Winchester rifle, Carson fired.

Sanders, who was a man of middle years with receding reddish-brown hair, dropped the rifle, clutched at his chest and then performed a sort of dance across the room. He turned wild eyes on Carson, reached for a bowie knife at the back of his belt. It fell from his fingers as Carson shot him again.

Candice had begun to scream; acrid gunsmoke rolled across the room.

'Get her to shut up,' Carson ordered. 'We don't know how near the others might be. Then grab your coats. We're leaving — now.'

'Come on, Candice,' Carson heard Ruth say as he toed Sanders' dead body. 'We've got to make this swift and silent.' A good woman, Ruth. A sturdy, practical woman, Carson thought, somewhat revising his earlier opinion of the elder sister.

'Are there any saddles around?' Carson asked.

'Only the two that I saw earlier,' Ruth answered. 'Bill Saxon and Lou took those. They were riding Sanders' saddle horses.'

'Then it will have to be bareback on the bay horses — can you handle them?'

'Mister,' Candice said, buttoning her coat. She had finally calmed down enough to speak. 'You are talking to two Nine-Slash-Seven girls. We were riding bareback before we were big enough to heft a saddle.'

'Fine, that'll help,' Carson said. He asked Ruth Prince, 'Did you tell her?'

Ruth shook her head. 'There hasn't been time.'

'Tell me what?' Candice demanded, looking from one to the other.

'Wesley Short is in the inn in town, wounded. He came all this way to find you, Candice.'

'Oh,' was all Candice managed to gulp, but she seemed energized now. There's nothing like having a new dream to replace the one that's fragmented itself.

Outside there was still no sign of Lou Weathers or Bill Saxon. Maybe they could make their getaway clean. As Carson gathered up his gray horse again, the two girls scurried to the lean-to. Selecting two of the team bays, they were back astride in minutes, guiding the horses easily, true to Candice's boast.

'Where now?' Ruth asked, looking with doubtful eyes at the sky and the shack where Sanders lay dead. Carson replied tersely:

'Away.'

Carson let the girls on the unequipped bay horses lead the way down the trail, following in case they should encounter some trouble with their mounts. It had begun to snow again — lightly but steadily. His own tracks were still easy enough to make out on the road, and the women followed these without a lot of effort.

It was going to work; he had gotten

the women away, Carson told himself.

That self-congratulatory mood lasted all of another minute. They followed the trail along an outward curve and suddenly a man's voice boomed out from behind them. It only took a glance to reveal the two mounted men there to be Lou Weathers and Bill Saxon.

Weathers had a gun drawn, but he hesitated to use it. Now Saxon drew his own pistol and even at this distance Carson could see the deadly intent in the thief's eyes. Saxon was not so averse to firing near the women as his friend was. Whatever game Saxon was playing, it was obvious he did not intend to lose it at this late stage.

A lone shot was loosed, racketing down the long, rocky slope.

11

Candice Prince looked back with terror in her young eyes. Ruth looked to Carson for instructions.

'Just keep moving,' Carson yelled out, halting his horse. He drew his rifle from the scabbard, watching to make sure that Ruth and Candice were following his order, then turned the gray on the narrow trail and sighted at the first man rushing toward him.

Lou Weathers was firing now that the women were gone, but he was shooting from a charging horse while Carson had halted and steadied his aim. Lou Weathers was a big target and, with the Winchester, Carson could hardly miss.

He saw the rider throw up his hands and sag, falling from his saddle. One of Lou's boots got caught in the stirrup, and his charging horse dragged him along for a quarter of a mile or so over the rocky ground before it slowed, halted and turned in a confused circle.

Carson tried to train his rifle sights on the second kidnapper, Bill Saxon, but Saxon was a schemer, not a fighter. As soon as he saw Lou Weathers knocked out of the saddle, Saxon's courage seemed to flag. He was now thinking only of escape.

Already Carson had lost sight of the thief as he rode back around a curve in the snaking road. There was nothing for it but to pursue the blond man. There was only one person left who could have Julian Prince's stolen money — the man who had plotted all this in the first place.

Carson started his gray horse back up the trail as the snow began to fall in earnest, the wind behind it, stinging his cheeks and blurring the mountain trail.

The wind did not abate; the snowfall did not diminish. By the time Carson Banner reached the Sanders cabin again, there was already enough new snow on the ground that he could see clearly that Saxon had not ridden that way. Saxon could have no hope that Sanders was still alive. Not if Carson had the women. The house was virtually impregnable, set up as it was. There was no escape once it was entered.

Bill Saxon had continued on, retracing his route up the western trail. Did that mean the man meant to return to Tumble Oaks? Carson could think of no reason why Saxon would do that. He had no allies left in town; he cared nothing about Candice or what happened to her. No — Saxon had the money and he meant to make a dash into the wild country. Probably he had noticed a secondary trail leading off of this one on his trip to town. Carson, who had no idea where he was going, had to take things slow in this weather, watching for dangerous stretches of road and straining his eyes to follow the recent tracks of Saxon's horse.

At the moment Saxon was gaining much ground on Carson, but it would not continue. Carson doubted that

Saxon would show any more courage in open country than he had previously. He had his money and he meant to live well and safely on it. Getting into a shooting fray was no way to achieve his goal.

There was no telling where Saxon meant to go, but Carson would be on his heels. He was too close to success to consider relenting. He had achieved a half of what he set out to do. He would trust Wesley Short, not that badly injured, to protect the women for now. Carson had a purse he meant to capture for the old man who rightfully owned it.

The trail suddenly forked. A narrower path deviated from the road, leading sharply upward into the dense ranks of snow-shrouded pine trees. Saxon had ridden that way. Carson paused at the fork in the road for a minute to allow his horse to blow and to examine the verge of the forest for any possible ambush. Then he started on again, grimly.

They just don't pay me enough for

this kind of work, he thought with a rueful smile. No, they didn't — that was true enough — but no one had twisted his arm, forced him to take the job.

Carson continued plodding his way through the rampaging storm.

He only here and there saw sign of another horse having passed. This was back among the tall blue pine trees where the snow had not gathered so quickly. Where was Saxon headed? The thief had no way of knowing this territory any better than Carson did, which was to say, not at all.

That was not totally true, Carson realized with a flash of inspiration. Bill Saxon did know a little of the area, a place of refuge, but would he dare to return there?

The mansion of Sterling March stood in isolation not half a day's ride ahead of them. It would take some gall to return to the beer baron's palatial house, but perhaps even now Saxon was concocting some fantastic story to convince Ben Howell that he needed to stay there once more. Some story that would undoubtedly paint Carson in a bad light. There were a dozen possible variations on the story, Carson decided.

Would Saxon be believed? Who could guess? The thing was that Saxon, a professional conman, believed it would work in his desperation. If he did gain admittance to the March house — and they had a history of never turning a needy traveler away — he would not have to fear being gunned down in the house.

As Ben Howard had made perfectly clear on their last visit to the house, they also had a history of discouraging violence in the place with whatever measures it took to maintain the peace.

Again Carson Banner knew this was all speculation on his part, but then, where else would a running jackal with no winter gear and no understanding of the north country go?

The tracks he followed throughout

the day led him to believe that he had guessed right. The horse Bill Saxon was riding was being guided in nearly a straight line, directly toward the March house — or as directly as the terrain would allow.

The land again dipped down into a narrow wooded valley. Carson felt that by now Saxon had probably ridden the speed out of the blue roan — one of Sanders' two horses — and that on his plodding but steady gray horse he was likely making up ground. He wondered if he could catch up with Saxon before he reached his destination, knowing that once the thief had taken refuge there, there would be no chance of administering justice.

The protective Ben Howard with his big Colt Walker would not allow any such goings-on.

Carson approached the stand of tall pines as the wind whipped the heavy, falling snow around him, buffeting him. It was as if a screen had been drawn across the world now — a cold, concealing screen. He had lost Saxon's tracks, but the man figured to continue in a straight line as he had been doing. Why wouldn't he? Where else had he to go?

Lightning crackled from within the nest of heavy, surrounding clouds, spiking across the sky, followed by the close boom of thunder.

The second boom was not that of nature. A weapon had been fired from within the forest verge, and Carson felt the gray horse shudder beneath him, then begin a headfirst collapse toward the ground. Carson kicked free, firing back three times at the unseen rifleman as he fell and rolled into the snow. A second rifle bullet shredded the meat of Carson's left shoulder as he was falling.

The horse flailed briefly in a death run and then lay still. Carson cursed himself. He had again let his speculation, his guesses command his actions. He had not figured Saxon to stand and fight, but that was exactly what the blond adventurer had chosen to do.

Carson lay just within the perimeter of the trees. The pines offered some protection from the raging wind, some shield from the heavily falling snow, but little enough. He lay flat on his belly for long minutes, moving only to thumb fresh cartridges into his Colt's cylinder.

There were no further shots, but that meant nothing. Perhaps Saxon was exhibiting more patience than Carson had given the man credit for. It was time to move. It was that or die against the frozen earth buried by new snow, the life force leaking out of him. The wind had grown stiffer yet. It twisted whistling through the trees, setting the tall pines to moaning and swaying.

Carson got slowly into a crouched position and then darted for the cover of the nearest pine, a huge specimen eight feet in diameter. He paused there, listening, peering around the trunk of the tree. He had only a rough idea of where Saxon had fired from, but then the man might have moved by now.

Carson moved toward the spot he

believed the sniper fire had come from, running in a crouch, darting from tree to tree. Still there was no sound but the whining progress of the wind through the forest. No shots followed him, no horse pounded away through the woods. Carson continued forward, moving stealthily, his pistol held high and cocked.

Fifty yards farther on Carson again encountered Bill Saxon.

The blond man lay sprawled on his back against the snow, the blood from his body staining it pink. One of Carson's off-hand shots, fired as he fell from the gray's back, had tagged the thief, put an end to his run.

Drawing in his breaths heavily, Carson stood for a moment, hovered over Saxon. He did not have to worry, Bill Saxon would not rise again — his days of troublemaking had come to an end. Farther back, among the trees, Carson spotted the young blue roan that Saxon had been riding. The horse stood in an awkward posture, and nearing the animal, Carson could see that it was injured. Its right-front leg had gone lame.

Probably that was the only reason a desperate Bill Saxon had tried the ambush. Holstering his pistol, Carson searched Saxon's saddle-bags. The money was there — some in gold, but mostly in paper currency. He didn't try to count it then. Carson stroked the uneasy, pained blue roan's muzzle. Was the little horse even capable of carrying him, or at least transporting the saddle-bags farther? Carson's shoulder, which had been raw with fiery pain moments ago, was now nearly immobilized by cold. He could use all the help he could get.

It was a minute before Carson realized that he was not alone in the forest.

The beast made only small, snuffling sounds as it prowled around Saxon's body. When Carson turned it seemed as if the yellow eyes of the old, scruffy wolf were fixed directly on his in warning.

What now? Try to kill the wolf so that

it did not make a meal of Saxon's body when nothing else in all the world or beyond had any use for it? Missing a shot, or failing to make it a killing one, could find the snarling wolf on top of Carson, fighting a desperate fight that he could not win. Silently, carefully, his eyes on the old lone wolf, Carson reached for the reins of the blue roan. Turning the limping horse's head, he started out of the forest, leaving the wolf to its found wealth, Saxon to his ignoble reward.

Carson tried to put the fate of Bill Saxon out of his mind as he trailed north aboard the hobbling horse. The blue roan could not travel at more than a walking speed, and even that seemed too much for it. It frequently mis-stepped and stumbled. Carson knew he was not going to make it on his own, however, and so he urged the little pony on, mentally apologizing to the animal, which had done nothing to deserve this torment, but only tried to serve men as well as it could.

189

The day continued to grow colder, darker. Hot blood had begun to seep again from Carson Banner's shoulder. At times he could see nothing ahead as the storm continued to rampage. The pony stumbled again, and out of pity and a realization that there was little choice, Carson slipped to the ground to wade through the calf-high snow, leading the blue roan.

How far had he come? He could not say. How far was there left to go? Could he find shelter before the hideous, frozen night fell? He doubted that he could survive a night out in this weather. Travel was perilous enough now. If the overnight temperature dropped another thirty or forty degrees a man without shelter, a fire, blankets would have no chance of seeing the dawn.

Carson guessed that it was already near to sundown. The sky was very dark, but a strange sunset light seeping in through some fissure in the clouds painted the falling snow a deep mauve. That display of color lasted only a few minutes, and then he was alone in the darkness again. The little horse stumbled and Carson waited while it gathered itself again. If turning the horse loose would have done it any good, he would have, but there was no more chance for a lone horse in the frozen wilderness than there was for a lone man.

Carson staggered on, the falling snow heavy across his body. He paused, blinked and started on again. Something he had seen . . . he paused and looked again, wiping the snow from his eyes. He was looking directly at a single star which somehow had enough brilliance to beam down through the turbulent darkness.

Except that it was no star. The bulky shoulder of a huge house showed itself against the sky. Within it a light glowed. Carson gathered up the pony's reins once again and staggered on.

12

To Carson Banner it seemed that he was marching along a dark, frozen treadmill, failing to progress toward the house, which had to be that of Sterling March. There were no other structures around in this high mountain country. He waded on through the snow, going sometimes to his waist, trying to lead the horse. Trying to stay alive, alert as the blood slowly leaked from him. It would be ironic if he were found in the spring only steps from the house. Found like Curt and Abel Yardley would be after the spring sun had worked its magic.

Carson slogged on toward the lantern in the window of the big house, seeming to get no nearer, but only weaker as he went. It seemed hours, days, years later before he mounted the front porch to the March mansion, his legs wobbly, his head spinning, his shoulder aching horribly. He had the saddle-bags over his shoulder, nothing else. The mournful blue roan stood with its head bowed, tail turned to the wind. Carson didn't have the strength to aid the horse any further. Perhaps Jingo could be roused.

Carson knocked on the heavy door, leaning against the wall for support. It did not open for long minutes and when it did Carson staggered inside eagerly, feeling the welcome warmth of the place wash over him.

It was Ben Howard who had opened the door for Carson. The young man had the big Colt Walker in his hand. Carson smiled crookedly, nodding at the gun.

'You won't be needing that, Ben,' Carson Banner said, and then he pitched forward, going to the hardwood floor face-first.

★ ★ ★

'Where am I?' Carson asked the first shadow that he met. He was lying in a place which was somehow familiar. The shadow spoke.

'Used to be my room — it's yours for the time being, I guess,' Elijah Tuttle said.

'I made it, then,' Carson murmured. When his head began to clear a little he again looked at Lige, who was sitting in a bedside wooden chair wearing a new pair of jeans and a white, long-sleeved shirt. The old man was also shaven.

'You look fine, Lige,' Carson said.

'They take care of me around here,' the old mountain man said. 'Besides, Virginia is constantly on me to keep myself clean.'

'The redhead, you mean,' Carson said, recalling Lige's nurse.

'That's the one.' Lige smiled shyly. 'I guess she's kind of adopted me. I work here now, you see, Carson. Not much to do right now, but I help Jingo mind the stock. When the weather turns I guess I'll be a yard hand.'

'No more gold panning?' Carson asked.

'No more panning, no more trapping.'

194

Lige fell into thoughtful silence briefly. 'I guess I was slowly killing myself out there, Carson, and didn't even realize it.'

'So you intend to stay here. For how long?'

'As long as they'll have me. I got me a cottage out in the back, like Jingo's. Real nice little place.' Lige rose from his chair, his face concerned. 'Don't do that, Carson! I saw you starting to stretch your arms. That hole you've got in you isn't healed yet, won't be for some time.'

'I need to find out what happened to the Prince sisters. Is there any way someone could get through to Tumble Oaks?'

'Don't think so,' Lige replied. 'Can't see how. But we had that three-day thaw last week, and if that Wesley Short is any kind of clever, I'd imagine he has those girls back home to Daddy by now.'

'Last week?' Carson said in confusion. 'A three-day thaw, you say?'

'You pretty much slept through it,' Lige told him, getting to his feet.

'It doesn't seem possible!' A thought returned to Carson with a jolt. His head came up abruptly. 'When I got here I was carrying some saddlebags . . . '

'The ones with Julian Prince's money in them, you mean? No need for concern. Ben Howell put them in the big safe in Sterling March's office. The money couldn't be any safer in a bank.'

'That's a relief,' Carson said, letting his head fall back on to his pillow.

'Sure,' Lige said, patting Carson's good shoulder. 'All you have to worry about for now is getting well. It's snowing again outside anyway — a grand-daddy of a storm. You couldn't go anywhere if you wanted to.'

'Sit down again, Lige. Stay and talk with me awhile longer.'

'Can't do that,' Lige said. 'I've got a few chores to do. I was just watching you while your nurse had herself some supper.'

'My nurse?' Carson asked in confusion.

196

'You mean Virginia has been forced to sit with me, too?'

A voice at the doorway said, 'Not hardly, cowboy.' Daisy stepped into the room, her blue eyes wide and merry. 'Are you still mad at me?' she asked.

Carson studied the pretty young blonde, shook his head and answered, 'No, I'm not, Daisy. I don't think I ever really was.'

'That's good,' Daisy said, taking the chair that Lige had vacated. 'Well, what's for excitement today? Do you want to take your bath or watch me knit?'

'Doesn't matter — whatever the schedule says. Just so long as you're going to stick around.'

'Oh, I'm sticking around,' she told him. 'It's my job, isn't it? Besides, I'm not going to be that easy to get rid of this time.'

And Carson found himself believing her.

We do hope that you have enjoyed reading this large print book.

Did you know that all of our titles are available for purchase?

We publish a wide range of high quality large print books including:
Romances, Mysteries, Classics
General Fiction
Non Fiction and Westerns

Special interest titles available in large print are:
The Little Oxford Dictionary
Music Book, Song Book
Hymn Book, Service Book

Also available from us courtesy of Oxford University Press:
Young Readers' Dictionary
(large print edition)
Young Readers' Thesaurus
(large print edition)

For further information or a free brochure, please contact us at:
Ulverscroft Large Print Books Ltd.,
The Green, Bradgate Road, Anstey,
Leicester, LE7 7FU, England.
Tel: (00 44) **0116 236 4325**
Fax: (00 44) **0116 234 0205**

BLIZZARD JUSTICE

Randolph Vincent

After frostbite crippled the fingers of his gun hand, Isaac Morgan thought his days of chasing desperadoes were over. But when steel-hearted Deputy US Marshal Ambrose Bishop rides into town one winter evening, aiming to bait a trap for a brutal gang which has been terrorizing the border, Morgan's peace is shattered. For after the lawman's scheme misfires, and the miscreants snatch the town judge's beautiful daughter Kitty, Bishop and Morgan must join forces to get her back.

DYNAMITE EXPRESS

Gillian F. Taylor

Sheriff Alec Lawson has come a long way from the Scottish Highlands to Colorado. Life here is never slow as he deals with a kidnapped Chinese woman, moonshine that's turning its consumers blind, and a terrifying incident with an uncoupled locomotive which sees him clinging to the roof of a speeding train car. When a man is found dead out in the wild, Lawson wonders if the witness is telling him the whole truth, and decides to dig a little deeper . . .

HANGING DAY

Rob Hill

Facing the noose after being wrongfully convicted of his wife's murder, Josh Tillman breaks out of jail. Rather than go on the run, he heads home, determined to prove his innocence and track down the real killer. But he has no evidence or witnesses to back up his story; his father-in-law wants him dead; a corrupt prison guard is pursuing him; and the preacher who speaks out in his defence is held at gunpoint for his trouble . . .

APACHE SPRING

J. D. Kincaid

When a stagecoach bound for El Paso is held up by bandits, all but one of the passengers are massacred. Young Lizzie Reardon, a teacher about to take up a post in the school at Burro Creek, is the sole survivor — but, as she has seen the attackers' faces, she is now their target. Deputy Sheriff Frank McCoy joins forces with the famous Kentuckian gunfighter Jack Stone to defend her — but will they succeed?